Hiding Behind The Couch Series

Perfect Tenor

by
Debbie McGowan

Beaten Track
www.beatentrackpublishing.com

Perfect Tenor
First published 2021 by Beaten Track Publishing
Copyright © 2021–2023 Debbie McGowan

Paperback ISBNs:
978 1 78645 528 4
978 1 78645 551 2
eBook ISBN: 978 1 78645 529 1

Cover Design by Debbie McGowan

Beaten Track Publishing,
Burscough, Lancashire.
www.beatentrackpublishing.com

Contents

1: Advent Sunday

Pete

THE BELL CEASED its toll as Pete dived through the vestry doors, panting and tearing off his jacket. It was astonishing he could hear the bell at all over the rapid thrum of his heart and his mum's mantra, *more haste, less speed*, running on a loop in his ears, not that he'd ever understood what it meant. Nor did he care when the procession had already begun. He'd have to sneak into the gallery after the event and hope no-one—namely, Mr. Lewis the choirmaster, organist and all-round terroriser—noticed.

Pete threw on his alb as he belted up the stairs and cracked open the door, stopping before it hit the hinge-creak point so he could watch and wait for his opportunity. This was why he hated weekends on call. On the one hand, there were few emergencies in local authority recycling; on the other, the absence of such had fooled him into believing it would be pointless warning Mr. Lewis he might not make it to Mass. Still, he *had* made it, which, by the looks of things, was more than could be said for most of the parish.

Sliding into his spot at the right end of the second row, Pete had a clear view of the rest of the choir and congregation. It was a sorry sight. He'd been coming to church all his life and had joined the choir when he was seven, one of three boys amid a self-replenishing sea of warbling older women who formed the soprano section at Our Lady's. Now there were no boy sopranos at all, and Pete, these days a tenor, was the sole remaining member of the original trio—the only chorister under the age of forty, in fact, and that was OK. What wasn't OK was being one of only eight choristers— a bass, two tenors, four altos and a soprano—at this morning's Mass, and on Advent Sunday too.

"Flu," Norman, the other tenor, murmured a bit too close to Pete's ear for comfort. He was a nice enough fella to sing alongside, but while most of the choir assumed he had chosen the single life, Pete knew different. A couple of years ago, Norman had invited him out for a drink, and Pete had said yes, regretting it before he'd finished his first pint. Aside from choir, they had zero in common, and Norman's enthusiasm for All Things Philately was about as interesting to Pete as decomposing mulch. When Norman later asked if he'd be his plus-one for a Christmas works do, Pete had gently turned him down, explaining he'd be at his brother's, *waaaay* out of town, which was true—and the first Christmas in years he'd been glad of the reason. Next time they saw each other was the first choir practice of the new year, and they'd carried on as usual. Neither had mentioned it since.

"At least we're all right, eh?" Norman whispered, tapping his upper arm. Pete nodded, already singing the 'Kyrie', which Norman joined on the first 'Eleison'. They'd bumped into each other at the flu jab clinic—hurray for being asthmatic. Or not. Pete had been a poorly kid, but he hadn't had an attack since his teens, and that one was his own fault for trying smoking. Still, it got him his annual flu jab, so he wasn't complaining.

Strange, though, that the flu had knocked out half the congregation when most of them were eligible for the jab on age alone. Not so for Pete's supervisors, which was why both had called in sick this weekend, and pre-Christmas clear-outs made for busy recycling centres. He'd brought in a couple more staff on overtime, and he had his phone with him. That was the best he could do because he wasn't missing church for work, not in Advent.

With the 'Kyrie' over, the littluns, no more than a half dozen of them, went off to Sunday school, leaving the adults to sniffle their way through uninspiring readings and a sermon that was dreary even by Father Benson's standards. Pete scanned the congregation, staring at the backs of his parents' heads, both seeming rapt, but then his dad turned, looked up at the gallery and grinned, as did Pete, at the shared memory of Pete's first full Mass when he'd asked why the sermon was so boring, to which his dad had said it was the law and also why they kept the church so cold and uncomfortable—so people didn't nod off before the priest was done.

Tedious as it could be, Pete loved the familiarity and routine of Sunday mornings. At church, he didn't have to think about what to say or how to behave. Following the order of Mass was something he'd done for so long, it was more natural to him than the ritual of shaving or almost anything else he had to do.

That was also what his schoolfriends had never understood. He didn't go to church because his parents made him; he went because he wanted to. Even on Christmas Day, when the entire family descended on his brother's local church, the simple fact of being in God's house brought him enough peace and comfort to see out the toughest week—Christmas with the family was… a challenge—and he jonesed for it when, for whatever reason, he had to miss a Sunday. Did he believe in God? He wasn't sure, but he couldn't deny what he felt when he worshipped with others, as if their communal songs connected them to a higher presence.

That state of elevated spirituality had to be the reason Pete didn't see their choirmaster advancing on him after Mass, and by the time he did notice, it was too late to flee without it being obvious.

"Mr. Davenport! A word if I may."

Pants. "Mr. Lewis, I'm sorry about being late. I'm on—"

"Oh-ho-ho!" The man was like a garden rake and in his white robe was more 'cheap Hallowe'en ghost' than Santa, but he was positively jovial. "I'm sure you have a perfectly valid reason for your atypical tardiness. 'Tis by the by!" He waggled his hand in front of Pete's face. "I'd like to introduce you to Mr. Walker. Another tenor to swell our choral throng." Turning, Mr. Lewis hooked one of his spindly arms around the man hovering a couple of feet behind him, whom Pete also hadn't noticed until the man was propelled into his personal space.

"Hello." There was a glimmer of a shy smile and a searching glance half-hidden by the overhead light's reflection in his glasses. He must have noticed Pete's gaze shift to his hair—a sun-touched mid-brown—as he scooped back his curtain bangs and attempted that smile again. Pete's pulse took off.

"Hello." Now, for as much as he was both the youngest of seven *and* the least talkative, he was certain there were more words in the English language than 'hello'. Apparently, he'd forgotten them all.

"I'll let the two of you become acquainted," Mr. Lewis said. He was gone before Pete registered he'd spoken, and so had the rest of the congregation other than the astoundingly handsome Mr. Walker.

"Er, I'm Pete." Years of training thrust his arm forward, offering a handshake on his behalf.

"Byron." He bashfully accepted the handshake.

"You're a tenor." *Hazel eyes? Or brown? Can't really tell.* Pete sidestepped, shifting the position of the circular blobs of light so he could see past them. *Hazel.*

"I am. How about you?"

"Me too."

"Good, good."

Pete nodded along, resisting the urge to scratch his neck, and it had nothing to do with worrying he was making a bad first impression. Whoever's alb he was wearing—definitely not his—

4

the collar was rough as sandpaper. "So…have you just moved here, or…?"

"Sort of. I did my teacher training at the uni, so I've been here four years already, but this is my first term of teaching."

"What d'you teach?"

"Science."

"Which school?" Pete wanted to slap himself. He was asking because he was interested in knowing all there was to know about this new tenor whose gentle presence had him jelly-kneed, yet it felt more like an interrogation.

"Moor Croft."

"I went there."

"Did you?" Byron's eyes flitted to Pete's neck. "It's a good school." And again. He was blushing too.

"It is."

"How about you? What do you do?"

"Public servant." Pete poked his finger down his collar and tugged it away from his neck, which had become unbearably itchy. "Refuse disposal. I manage the recycling centres. Excuse me, but I need to go and take this off." Forget 'go'. The itch was now a burn, and Pete yanked the alb over his head right where he stood—in the aisle. The polyester mix crackled with static and set his hair on end as he emerged from the blue gown and peeled it away from his jumper, getting zapped in the process. He ran his fingers over the place where his neck was burning. It was hot and bumpy, and Byron was watching with concern.

"How bad is it?" Pete asked.

"Pretty bad. Allergic reaction?"

"I think so." Sniffing the collar of the alb, he picked up a hint of cologne. "Serves me right for grabbing the wrong one." He was beginning to see his mother's point about 'more haste, less speed', not that he was allergic to many things, but perfumed stuff was generally what set off a reaction. "I've got antihistamines in my jacket in the vestry. Want to come and meet the others?"

"Great." Byron nodded enthusiastically but seemed a little reticent.

Pete set off, checking he didn't lose Byron along the way. "It shouldn't be too daunting. You probably noticed there weren't many of us this morning."

"How many are there usually?"

"Twenty, I think?" Pete had never counted. "There're five tenors—well, six now." He smiled over his shoulder. "I'm so happy you've joined us." He quickly faced forward again, no idea why he'd said that. Sure, he'd been thinking it, but he usually limited speaking his mind to his siblings, and even then only Charlie and Ed got the full, uncensored Pete.

Thankfully, his embarrassment over his openness subsided somewhat by the time they reached the vestry and he had to look Byron in the eye again. A couple of the women had left already, but the men were still there. Norman was fastening his duffle coat and glanced up briefly, then back down, then up again.

"Byron, this is Norman. A fellow tenor."

Norman smiled and extended a hand. "Nice to meet you." An odd something or other flashed across his face, but he quickly went back to fiddling with his toggles, so Pete couldn't be sure what it was. He hoped it wasn't jealousy. He moved on.

"And this is Bob." He gestured to the morning's sole bass, whom people said looked like a British bulldog, although Pete thought he had an uncanny likeness to a toad. Then again, Pete had also seen Bob performing his role of councillor, and politicians were a slimy bunch. Whatever, Byron got charming, kiss-a-baby Bob, but there was, Pete hoped, plenty of time for Byron to get to know them all better.

"Who's this then?" One of the three remaining women dodged around Bob and beamed a 100-watt grin their way.

"Carol, meet Byron—our new tenor. Byron, this is Carol. She's an alto, as is Mary over there." He'd raised his voice for the last part, as Mary was in her nineties and her hearing wasn't so good. "And Joan—" he nodded at the woman helping Mary with her coat "—is a soprano."

"Hiya, love," Joan called across. Byron raised his hand in acknowledgement. The poor guy looked overwhelmed.

"Right. Antihistamines." Byron was between Pete and the cupboard, and as Pete moved to pass in front of him, Byron stepped forward. After a few seconds of awkward dancing, Pete made it to his jacket and patted the pockets until he heard the crinkle of plastic. Extracting one of the little pills, he swallowed it dry and gladly returned the alb to its hanger. As an afterthought, he checked the name tag and took a startled step back. "Ugh. It's John's."

"Who?" Byron said.

"Hm?" Pete shook off the creeps. "Sorry. One of our tenors passed away in the summer, and that was his robe."

"Ah! Death cooties." Byron grinned, but then it must've dawned on him he was being insensitive because all the colour left his face in a rush.

Bob guffawed, his booming laughter as deep as his vocal range. "I like this lad," he said, clapping Byron on the shoulder and simultaneously manoeuvring him to the side. "See you on Thursday, God willing." Off he went, leaving the vestry door to thud loudly behind him.

"I'm so sorry," Byron said, staring at the floor as if urging it to disappear beneath his feet.

"No matter." Carol gave him a smile as she, too, passed him by. "I think you'll fit in nicely, eh, Pete?" She winked conspiratorially and disappeared into the church beyond. Pete stared after her, wondering how on earth she'd sussed him so quickly. Granted, she'd known him most of his life, but if it was that obvious to her, then—

"Do you?" Byron asked.

7

Slowly venting a breath, Pete turned Byron's way, intending to avoid eye contact. Instead, their gazes locked tighter than a council refuse truck on a wheelie bin. Not the greatest analogy, but that was Pete's life. "Do I what?"

"Think I'll fit in?"

"Oh! Yeah, I do." In the distance, beyond the moment, Pete heard the vestry door close again and realised Norman had left without saying goodbye.

2: Practice Makes...

Byron

IT HADN'T TAKEN long for Mr. Lewis to show his true colours—Byron had been warned by at least three different people what to expect. Within minutes of the start of his first practice with Our Lady's choir, the man had gone into a full-blown tantrum, as if the absentees had caught flu purely to spite him.

The rest of the choir seemed pretty approachable—even Councillor Bob, whom Pete said had a temper on him. Then there was Norman. Despite the two of them hitting it off on something of a wrong foot and for no reason Byron could fathom, Norman was well respected by the other choristers—not least of all Pete—so when he proposed putting a couple of tenors and altos on soprano parts, Byron backed his play...and blotted his copybook, as his grandad would have said.

His grandad had played the organ back home, and his gran had been one of those hardy altos common to all choirs, including Our Lady's. By Byron's third Thursday-night practice, the numbers had swelled from the eight on Advent Sunday to a 'massive' fourteen, half of whom were altos—the full complement. The basses were at half strength—Councillor Bob and Walter Claus, who actually was Santa at the Christmas fête every year without recourse to fake facial hair or body padding. Those two mighty basses could've been sitting on separate continents for all the notice they took of each other, whereas the four tenors—Pete, Norman, Byron and Fabio, a sixty-something Pavarotti-alike—were chatterboxes and had been shushed countless times. Meanwhile, poor old Joan was still singing solo soprano.

Disgruntled as Mr. Lewis was by mere tenors telling him how to run the choir he'd been in charge of for who knew how long— Pete was twenty-five, same age as Byron, and said he'd only known Mr. Lewis—his choice was to tell Father Benson there would be no choir for the last Sunday of Advent, something he'd never had to do before, or go with Norman's suggestion. He didn't go down without a fight, though.

"Mr. Walker, seeing as you enjoy standing up to be counted, you can take the first verse of 'The King Shall Come'. Ready?" Without giving any of them a chance to find it in their hymnals, he struck up the introduction noisily on the much-battered, twangy church hall piano.

Luckily, Byron remembered the first two lines from having sung them so often at church back home, so he managed to sing those while frantically flicking through the pages and made it by the skin of his teeth, which was good in a way. It distracted him from wondering how Pete felt about the new boy being given a solo or what he'd think of Byron's performance. Granted, they'd sung next to each other for two practices and two Masses already, but there had been no pressure to do anything more than hit the right notes.

With relief, he reached the end of the first verse mistake-free and relaxed into it a little when the others joined in for the second verse. It was a good choice of hymn in the circumstances, being in unison and not technically difficult. Even so, Byron wasn't happy about having been put on the spot, particularly as, when they reached the end of the third verse, Mr. Lewis glowered at him over his half-moons and said only, "It'll do."

At Byron's side, Pete huffed, turning it into a cough when Mr. Lewis's glower shifted his way.

"'Wake, O Wake' next. Mr. Davenport, Mr. Walker and you three—" he motioned with a sharp jerk of the head to three of the altos "—go and stand with Mrs. Carson." That was Joan. He gave them just enough time to move before he started playing. The first verse was again in unison, and it sounded OK. The second was where things could have come unstuck, with five of them on a part they'd never sung before, but Joan was strong and didn't actually need them squawking alongside her soaring operatic soprano.

'Wake, O Wake, And Sleep No Longer' had *long* verses, so it was as well Mr. Lewis cut them off after the second, even if he did leave it until they were midway through a hearty *Glory, glory, sing the angels* that fizzled away faster than candy floss in the rain. After that, they went through a few standard carols, the final selection to be decided on Christmas morning, depending on who made it, and at last Mr. Lewis dismissed them to enjoy what was left of their Thursday evening in the pub next to the church.

Byron almost made it to the door before Mr. Lewis called him back. The others had stepped outside already and stopped.

"I'll catch you up," Byron said, and they moved off again. Hoping he hadn't imagined Pete's reluctance to abandon him, he turned his attention to Mr. Lewis.

"You seem to have settled in well, Mr. Walker."

"Yes, I have, thank you."

Mr. Lewis's answering grunt was as good as saying *don't thank me yet*, followed by, "See you Sunday. Don't be late," and a jangle of keys to hurry Byron along. Byron did so with gladness and no idea what the point had been of holding him back, other than for Mr. Lewis to reassert his authority.

Outside, the air was cold and dry and mildly sulphurous with the smoke from nearby chimneys. That was a big difference between this town and where Byron had grown up. People here still had open fires, and on a dark December evening, with the glow of Christmas lights in almost every window and muffled sounds of merriment from the pub next door, Byron was deeply moved and a little nostalgic. Christmas had always been his favourite festival.

Stepping into the warmth of the pub brought a wholly different sensory experience—the rich, hoppy aromas of cask ales mixed with warm whiskey, the hum of conversations nestled against Christmas pop music, and the sight of Pete Davenport, who was standing at the bar and acknowledged Byron with a smile that set his insides fluttering.

"What are you drinking? Orange juice? Coke? Or can I tempt you with a glass of the hard stuff?"

"How hard are we talking?" Byron asked, the double entendre completely unintentional. He did his best to pretend it wasn't one, but evidently, his face was as red as it felt because Pete grinned at him.

"Bitter shandy? It's a school night, after all."

Byron laughed, still embarrassed, although it helped that over the past fortnight, they'd established they were both more socially awkward than the average person. With minimal chance of interaction at church, that was about as far as they'd got. "Go on," he said. "Not shandy, though. A straight pint of bitter."

"Bitter, OK." Pete relayed that to the landlady—Mrs. O'Shea—who was surly and scary enough to be Mr. Lewis's twin, although perhaps she needed to be, running a pub like the Blue Anchor. According to Councillor Bob, it was a bit rough and as such in an ideal location—next to a church and opposite the police station.

"*If that doesn't deter them, they can pop next door and take their chances with the man upstairs,*" Bob had said with one of his chesty chuckles that could've blown out the votives from the gallery.

Pete paid for their pints and handed one over, eyes trained on his beer. "Does it have to be straight?"

"Eh?" Byron took a sip, letting the dark liquid sit on his tongue, both to savour the taste and figure out what Pete meant.

"A straight pint of bitter, you said." Pete glanced up and away again. A warm bloom of pink spread along his cheekbones. "Peanuts. I fancy some peanuts."

"Oh!" Byron had been wondering how they might initiate that conversation. He'd tried with a tentative 'anyone special?' after their first choir practice, which Pete had answered with a flat 'no', so Byron had left it alone, assuming he'd either hit a nerve or was barking up the wrong tree.

"Do you want any bar snacks?" Pete asked.

"No, I'm fine, thanks." He studied Pete's profile. His ear was pink now, too, and there was a telltale dent in the lobe. "Are both your ears pierced?"

"Yeah. Why?"

"Just wondering."

Pete turned to check Byron's ears. "Yours aren't."

"God, no." He shuddered at the idea.

"You don't like piercings?"

"I do on other people. I have zero pain tolerance."

"It doesn't hurt that much."

"Happy to take your word for it." He took another sip of beer, swallowed, said, "No, it doesn't have to be straight. In fact, I'd prefer it wasn't."

"Same," Pete said.

So that was that, then. Byron wasn't sure what to do with it yet, but there was no rush. He wasn't going anywhere.

Once Pete had his peanuts, they went and sat at a table near the other choristers, who were heavily engrossed in a communal grumble about their illustrious leader.

"I still can't believe he threw that solo at you," Pete said. "You were brilliant, by the way."

"Thanks!" And now Byron was blushing again. He pressed on, hoping Pete hadn't noticed, although the curious tilt of his head said otherwise. "You'd have even more trouble believing how nice he was to me at parents' evening when he found out I was in the choir back home."

"He can be a charmer when he wants," Carol interjected and gained multiple grunts of agreement, which confirmed they had no chance of talking privately here. "And I'm with Pete. You've got the voice of an angel."

"Oh, yes!" said one of the other altos.

"That you have," said another.

"Lovely tone." And another.

Byron smiled politely at the gushing women, praying they'd go back to their conversation and leave him to enjoy his shame in peace. The church choir solo was nerve-wracking, but it was, by a long shot, the least of his worries.

There were reasons—too many to process—why Byron hadn't rocked up to join the church choir earlier or mentioned he was a musician on his teaching application form or at interview, and he'd planned on keeping it to himself. But then, at the first staff meeting, the department heads had outlined their plans for the year, and Byron's attention had drifted to all the assignments and observations he had to complete alongside attending parents' evenings and helping his students prepare for exams and the science fair and filling in university applications. He'd be busy. No time for extracurricular stuff, so he didn't need to listen. He'd stuck to that, too, until the head of music waxed lyrical about 'Carols by Candlelight', which turned out to be a community-wide event where all the local schools and churches came together for an evening of song, each providing one or two performances.

This year, Moor Croft's A' Level music class were performing one of their own arrangements, but with only a few days to go until the big event, their soloist had gone down with the flu. The rest of the ensemble were devastated, and there were no other students able or willing to step in. In desperation, the head of music turned to the staff, who pretty much en masse said *no thanks, it's Christmas break*, except there was no such thing for musicians, as well Byron knew. No matter how nervous he was about performing or how much work he had to do, he couldn't let down the students.

"Are you OK there?" Pete asked, and Byron nodded, even though his pulse was racing in anticipation of the weekend ahead, but it wasn't just nerves. He was excited. He hadn't performed a solo since his own high school days, and those were good memories.

"I was wondering..." He paused to check the women weren't still listening in. "Are you busy on Sunday evening?"

Pete grimaced. "Not exactly. I'll be at my brother's and probably bored out of my brains already. We go there every year."

"Not fun?"

"It's all right after a few shots of Christmas cheer." Pete raised his beer and took a swig in illustration.

Byron had the feeling it was a non-starter, but he had to ask. "Does your brother live nearby?"

"Sadly not. A few hours' drive away or else I'd be wherever you need me to be, for as long as you need me."

"Oh! Well, that's an offer for future consideration." He picked up his glass and tapped it against Pete's, an informal agreement to a rain check. He liked how their friendship was going, and if that's all they had, that was OK, although he couldn't deny he was attracted to Pete's quirky handsomeness. Perpetually ruffled dark hair, warm, brown, long-lashed eyes and clean-shaven baby face, he was somewhere between the cute one in a boy band and science nerd but with a tough, no-nonsense edge that probably came from being a manager.

"What's happening Sunday evening, by the way?" Pete asked.

"Carols by Candlelight."

"Really? That's late this year."

"Is it? It's my first one."

"Yeah, it's usually about halfway through the month—and on a Tuesday. Our choir used to take part, but Mr. Lewis fell out with the vicar at St. Mark's." Byron must've looked incredulous because Pete nodded and added, "I know! Reverend Osbourne gets on with everyone. That's what makes Carols by Candlelight so successful."

"We had nothing like that back home," Byron said. "Our church and the C of E are about a hundred yards apart, and there's a Methodist church a bit further along the street, but everyone sticks to their own denomination. Did I tell you my sister married a Protestant?"

"I didn't even know you had a sister."

"That's weird. I feel like all I do is talk about me."

"You don't, but I wouldn't mind if you did. So you've got a sister then?"

"Two, actually. One older than me, one younger—she's still at uni, just started her Master's in French. How about you? You have a brother, you said."

"Three brothers, three sisters."

"Whoa. That's, um…"

"A decent size for a Catholic family?" Pete suggested with a smirk.

"Yeah, that. Where do you rank in that lot?"

"I'm the afterthought."

"Ah, the baby."

"Hm." Pete frowned. "Ellie—the eldest—is sixteen years older than me, and Ben—whose house we endure Christmas at—is a year younger than Ellie. Then there's a four-year gap, then Charlie, Luke and Tilly, all two years apart, followed by a five-year gap, then Ed, who's two years older than me."

"And they'll all be there for Christmas, will they?"

"Oh, yeah. Along with assorted spouses and sprogs. Well, Charlie and Ed are both single as well."

"Uh-huh." Byron liked the sound of that 'as well' and spent a while pondering the possibilities. Was it too soon to arrange something for New Year's Eve? Or should he leave it until after the holidays? Of course, he was assuming Pete was interested when he could just be being friendly. Was he brave enough to ask?

"I wish I didn't have to go." Pete sighed, swirling his half-drunk beer around, but soon shook off his glumness. "I love that we all get together for Christmas, but I'm gutted I'll miss Carols by Candlelight."

"Do you usually go?"

"Nope." Pete grinned. "But I'd go for you."

"I'm honoured!"

"So are you singing or…?"

"I am."

"I always loved that about Moor Croft's school choir—that it's staff and students together."

"Yes, I love that too. Except…I'm not singing with the choir. I'm covering for a sixth-form soloist."

"Flipping heck! You're in hot demand! What are you singing?"

"'Gabriel's Message'. I'm playing cello too."

"You play cello? No way!"

"What? Do you play?"

"Sort of. I had lessons from when I was six till…I dunno. Fifteen, maybe. I kept meaning to get back to it, but then I left for uni, and my dad moved my cello into the loft. It's been there ever since."

"You should dig it out."

"I might just do that—after Christmas. How long have you been playing?"

"Same as you, pretty much, although I still dabble. Hey, we could have a jam sometime." Byron mentally crossed his fingers.

"You know I'll be awful, don't you?"

"No, you won't." Byron chanced a grin. "It's like riding a bike."

"Thanks for the vote of confidence, but I can't do that either." The way Pete's eyes lit up with mischief, he had to be tormenting.

Byron shook his head, laughing and wishing it wasn't school tomorrow because it was almost ten o'clock, and he could happily have stayed up all night chatting with Pete. Still, he stretched his beer as long as he could while they shared memories of their own school music lessons—awful—and what Moor Croft choir was singing on Sunday. All too soon, it was time to head home; Byron and Pete said their goodbyes to the other choristers, who were staying for another drink, and dawdled their way out of the pub.

"They record Carols by Candlelight, don't they?" Pete said.

"I believe so."

"Excellent. I won't completely miss you then." They reached the road and stopped next to Byron's clapped-out Yaris. "I really would love to be there."

"Me too," Byron said. "I mean, I'd love for you to be there because I'll already be there." He shut his eyes, berating himself for qualifying. It was obvious what he'd meant. On the plus side, embarrassment and a pint of beer was keeping him warm.

Pete laughed quietly. "So…cello jam after Christmas?"

"Only if you're up for it."

"Beats cranberry sauce."

"Terrible joke."

"No worse than the average Christmas cracker," Pete said as a hatchback stopped at the T-junction opposite and flashed its lights. "There's my lift. See you Sunday morning. Good night."

"Night!" Byron waited until Pete was in the car, which circled in the road, tooted and headed back the way it had come.

3: Good Tidings

Pete

PETE HAD OVERSLEPT. He'd known it for a good half hour before Ellie knocked on his bedroom door, but he was comfy and warm and keeping out of the way of the giggling and shouting going on downstairs. He'd never figured out why, whenever their mother shouted at Charlie and Ellie, the two of them got the giggles and ended up in even more trouble than they were in to start with.

A couple of minutes passed with no further demands from his oldest sister to "drag your stinking carcass out of your pit." Ignoring the likelihood he had been lulled into a false sense of lie-in security, Pete flipped to face the wall and threw an arm and a leg over his pillow. He really didn't want to get up for church. Well, no, that wasn't strictly true. Church was the only bit of the day he was excited for, but once that was done, they'd be heading down to Ben's. A three-hour drive followed by four days of *family fun*. Woohoo.

He was just drifting off when Ellie knocked on the door again.

"All right, already!" he shouted. He hadn't expected she'd give up, but he hated that her big-sister authority had him leaping out of bed as if his mattress had catapulted him. "For Christ's sake. I didn't even say I was going." Why would he when he went every Sunday?

He flung the door open and stomped past Ellie, ignoring her remark of, "Like you have a choice," but as he reached the bathroom door, she called, "Er, Pete?"

"What?" He looked back, and she thumbed in the direction of his bed.

"Who's...?"

"Why don't you go and say hello?" Pete suggested and dodged into the bathroom, grinning to himself. She probably wouldn't investigate further and was no doubt racing back downstairs to hurry their mother out the door so Pete's 'guest' could escape unseen, but Mr. Cuddles was here to stay.

It was pathetic, really. Pete hadn't realised how empty a bed could be until he and David had called time on their relationship, such as it was one. They'd met at university and had rooms in the same student house before getting together in their final year, but looking back, it had never felt permanent.

To be fair, neither of them had been particularly self-sufficient when they graduated, but while David flailed helplessly, Pete had found a job in a distribution centre and planned to rent a flat somewhere, the main problem being that he didn't have a permanent employment contract. Super-long, minimum-wage hours left him no time to look for a job more suited to the qualifications he'd spent the past three years and thousands of pounds of debt to obtain, never mind finding somewhere to live. His mum and dad had come to his rescue, suggesting he move back home until he could get a foot on his actual career ladder, and David had come too—on a temporary basis.

That was how Pete had sold it to his parents. They were housemates, and David would be moving on once he got his act together, which turned out to be true. No hard feelings, they'd parted ways quite amicably and still kept in touch. It had also given Pete the opening he'd needed to tell his parents he was gay, and even that hadn't been as bad as he'd feared. It helped that the Church had changed its stance on homosexuality, although it went without saying that Ellie had given him hell. She took the Church's view, essentially that it was OK to be gay but not to act on it, and by 'living with' David, he'd acted on it.

He knew all that. He'd confessed it all too, and Father Benson had accepted his confession in the way he had to, but outside of the confessional, he'd been amazingly supportive and, Pete suspected, talked his mum and dad around. It had been much harder for Charlie to come out to them as bisexual because they didn't understand why she couldn't 'just fall in love with a man'. Sadly and predictably, Father Benson hadn't come running to Charlie's aid, and Pete was uncomfortably aware he'd been given a pass because he was both male and an active member of the Church.

On which note, he needed to get a move on. Shower off, he slung a towel around his waist and tiptoed back to his room, on the way hearing his mum say, "It's almost half nine already. Is your brother up? I'm not being late for him if he isn't. He can make his own way." Clearly, his tiptoeing had been in vain, as the next second, she was stomping up the stairs.

"I'm up, Mum!" He poked his head out of the door to prove it.

"You're not even dry, let alone dressed! I'm not being late for you!"

"I—"

"And you haven't had breakfast—I bet you haven't packed yet either, have you?"

"Well—"

"You'll have to manage with a piece of toast. Where's your bag? I'll have to do it for you, as usual. I don't know..." And back down she went, muttering about how she'd thought now her children were adults, they'd look after themselves, but no, always leaving it to their mother, as if she didn't have enough to do already. At some point, she'd remember she'd ordered Pete and Charlie to share a suitcase to save space, and it was packed and in the car. Maybe one year, she'd even remember that Christmas was supposed to be a time for peace and restfulness. Still, he could do his part and not put any more stress on her.

It was a struggle while still damp, but he was dressed and heading for the stairs in less than two minutes. Then, for a laugh, he went back to his room and grabbed Mr. Cuddles. His timing couldn't have been more perfect. When he arrived in the kitchen, Ellie had her back to him, and he lobbed Mr. Cuddles right at her, whopping her on the shoulder.

"What in—" She whirled around with a face like thunder, then did a double-take. "Well! Would you look at the size of that!"

Before she could do a thing about it, Toby—her hyper two-year-old—dived head first from his chair onto Mr. Cuddles.

"Ah!" Charlie fell into a heap of giggles. "You thought... The pillow... Someone staying... Oh, God, it hurts."

"Charlotte!" their mother hollered. "Enough!"

Pete chuckled. This was so worth whatever punishment it brought later. "Ellie, meet Mr. Cuddles"—and to the pillow—"Mr. C, this is Ellie."

"Funny, you are not," Ellie grumbled.

Pete ignored her and crouched down to his nephew. "Good, isn't it?"

Toby nodded enthusiastically and rolled away, clinging to the six-foot-long pillow with both arms, much as Pete had been doing not ten minutes ago.

Ellie shook her head. "To think of the fortune I've spent on toys when I could've just got him one of those."

"It's the best thing I've ever bought," Pete said. "And it was great value. Free P and P. I could've got a second one for half price, but there's no room for a third."

"A wh...?" Ellie began, fizzling out when Charlie's giggling stopped as suddenly as if someone had hit a mute button.

The toaster pinged.

Charlie stared at Pete in disbelief, and it took his full effort not to laugh, now his festive spirit had kicked in. He shouldn't wind her up about her love life, but there was no way Ellie and their mum would understand what he'd said.

Their mum dumped a plate of toast and a glass of orange juice in front of him. "Get that down you, quick. We need to leave in ten minutes."

"That's ages yet."

"And you haven't shaved."

"Can't go to church with a beard," Charlie said.

"Why not?" Pete protested. "The disciples had beards." So did Byron, for that matter. Or long stubble, at least. Soft, no doubt.

"You're not a disciple. You're just a sad, single man who shares his bed with a man-size cushion."

"And Jesus." Pete gave Charlie a surreptitious wink.

"Peter! Get that toast eaten. Now!"

He took a bite and smirked at Charlie as he chewed, while Ellie wrestled Mr. Cuddles from Toby and propped it on the chair next to Pete's.

"We'll wait in the car," she said and followed their mother out the door.

Charlie stood to zip her jacket. "I hope your knees are in good shape this morning, matey."

"Why?"

"You've got some serious praying to do."

Pete shoved the rest of his toast into his mouth and took his plate to the sink, gulping down the glass of juice in one go. He covered his mouth and belched. "Excuse me."

"Excused. Come on, or she's gonna kill us."

Pete followed Charlie into the hallway and grabbed his coat. "You know there's only one reason I'm coming, don't you?"

"To keep Mum happy?"

"OK, two reasons."

"What's the other?"

"The new tenor."

"Who? Norman?"

Pete shoved Charlie out of the door. She only went to church for weddings, funerals and Christmas. "Norman joined the choir when I was still singing soprano, and he's really not my type. The new guy—"

"Vital statistics?"

"Twenty-five, single, brown hair, hazel eyes…"

"Hot?"

"They had to top up the font for the baptism last week. The water evaporated when he walked by."

"That hot, huh?" They put the conversation on hold to survey the car situation, both sharply drawing breath at their mother's snipe about it being 'a shame' Ellie's husband, who was a Buddhist, wasn't coming to church with them.

"He *is* coming for Christmas, isn't he?" Pete asked quietly.

Charlie shrugged. "Ellie says so. He's got to go back for Ollie on Boxing Day." Ollie was his son from his previous marriage. Charlie flinched at the bang of the driver's door being slammed shut and leaned a bit closer to Pete. "I'm not sure we'll fit in there with all those presents."

"No. I don't think we will. Your car?"

"Good idea." Charlie jangled her keys to tell Ellie and their mum what they were doing, whose matching expressions of disapproval made them look like a pair of scowling gargoyles.

"Oh, God. We're for the high jump now." Charlie unlocked the driver's door of her classic Golf, climbed in and reached over to let Pete in, and they were off, although they lost Ellie at the first set of traffic lights when she made it through and Charlie didn't, which was good. It gave them a chance to chat before their four days of conversation on approved topics only commenced, and Pete had been dying to ask what had happened to the woman Charlie had been dating, which was definitely not on the approved list, never mind that the rest of the family thought she was with Mike.

"Doesn't he mind you seeing other people?" Pete asked.

"Why would he? Neither of us are up for a relationship at the moment."

"Aren't you...you know?"

"Banging each other?"

"Er, yeah." Much as Pete loved their closeness and that they could be honest with each other, he was as shy as Charlie was outgoing and would never have used a phrase like that.

She glanced his way and laughed. "We are. But sometimes I just go over for footy and a beer."

"I could do with someone like that."

"You don't even watch footy."

"I would if someone made it worth my while."

"Norman, for instance?" Charlie teased.

"Norman," Pete repeated with a chuckle. "He asked me out. Did I tell you?"

"No?"

"It was a couple of years ago, to his work's Christmas do. I feel mean admitting it, but I was glad we do the whole family thing."

"And if the new guy asked?"

Pete sighed, no point in answering. They both knew the drill.

"It's stifling, isn't it?" Charlie said.

"That it is," Pete agreed. "Don't get me wrong, I love that we all spend Christmas together, but between Mum and Ellie stressing, Ben being a git, you and Dad drinking till you drop, the kids—"

"We do not!" Charlie protested, although she had no grounds to do so. "You can always join us."

"See, I would, except if Ben says, 'You're not old enough to drink,' one more time, I may do something I'll regret."

"Why d'you think me and Dad get drunk?" Charlie leaned forward so she could see past him to park outside the church, or not right outside. Judging by the row of cars in front of them, most people were over their flu. Pete glanced along the pavement to the church gate, the sight there making him wonder if he might be coming down with flu himself. Charlie must've noticed, as she looked where he was looking and mouthed an *oh*.

Pete cleared his throat and took off his seat belt.

"That him?" Charlie asked. "The new tenor?"

"Yeah. That's him." Pete made a fuss of checking his pockets and the foot well.

"Are you getting out? He's waiting for you."

"He's texting someone."

True, Byron had his phone in his hand, but his eyes were flitting between it and the car, and he was easily blushing as hard as Pete.

The driver's door thumped shut, and Pete realised he was alone in the car. He got out and locked up, taking a few deep, *more haste, less speed* breaths on his way over to Byron, impressed by how chill he sounded when he said, "Good morning."

"Morning!" Byron's smile was gorgeous. He seemed genuinely happy to see Pete, and he had lovely teeth. Was that a weird thing to notice? Pete didn't know. Didn't care much, either, other than he was staring and making Byron self-conscious. He stopped, sort of.

"Are you ready for your day of solos?" he asked.

"Nowhere near." They moved off together, towards the vestry. "I was just texting with the head of music about tonight. The guitarist's sick now too."

"Oh, no."

"Yeah. Luckily, there are a few sixth formers who play, so we're meeting up for a practice straight after church."

"Busy day, then."

"Uh-huh." They reached the vestry door, and Byron held it open for Pete.

"Thanks."

"Welcome. Hey, I was wondering..." Byron paused for them to say their good-mornings to the other choristers—Pete counted sixteen, which was good going—and then opened the cupboard, putting a door between them and peering over the top for Byron to finish what he was saying. "Maybe we could swap phone numbers so we can keep in touch over Christmas?"

"Yeah, great!" Pete had been wanting to ask for Byron's number but hadn't yet worked out if their friendship extended outside of church, although Byron *had* invited him to Carols by Candlelight. However, in his haste to show off Mr. Cuddles, he'd neglected to pick up his phone, which was still charging on his bedside table.

"One sec," he said. Ditching his alb, he darted through the door into the church and hurried over to the pew where Charlie, Ellie and his mum were all midway between sitting and kneeling. No surprise his dad hadn't arrived yet; same as every Christmas, he'd be 'getting the car ready for the long journey'. In other words, he was keeping out of Mum's way.

"Can I borrow your phone?" Pete asked Charlie. "I left mine at home."

She fished it out and handed it over. "What for?"

"To save his number. See you later." He speed-walked back to the vestry.

Byron was robed and doing a buzzy-bee warm-up to something of an audience. Between that and the call of, "Let's go, chaps," from Norman, they had to put their number exchanging on hold until after Mass, and it was a good one. The processional was amazing, despite Byron being so nervous his hair was damp with sweat by the end of his one-verse solo.

As for 'Wake, O Wake, And Sleep No Longer', the additional voices singing the melody along with the strengthened soprano section transformed what could be a very dreary, ploddy hymn into something truly special. Pete felt it in the swell of emotion that caught him unawares halfway through the second verse and saw it on the faces of the congregation, most of whom had turned their heads towards the gallery.

It was wondrous, and Pete didn't think he was the only one disappointed they missed out verse three, even if that was partly down to knowing his morning with Byron would soon be over; with no choir practice in Christmas week, they wouldn't see each other until next Sunday.

Of course, he'd overlooked one not-so-minor detail.

"When are you back from your brother's?" Byron asked as they walked the church path once more, taking the long route around the graves.

"Thursday, probably mid-afternoon by the time we get packed up. I'm gonna see if my sister will let me go in her car." He nodded in the direction of Charlie's Golf. Most of the other cars had gone already, including Ellie's. Byron's was two car-lengths in front of Charlie's.

"It *is* a GTi!" Byron said. "I thought it sounded like one the other night."

"That's some hearing you've got," Pete remarked.

"Musician's ears." Byron shrugged like it was a given but then smiled and admitted, "My dad used to have the same model, and I developed a knack for hearing him arrive home from work." He looked away, for no more than a second, but when he met Pete's gaze again, it seemed to take a bit of effort to reinstate the smile. "Are you free Friday evening?"

"I'm free Friday all day. Why?"

"Cello jam? I mean, we could do something else…"

Pete's stomach sank.

"Or forget it?" Byron suggested, misinterpreting Pete's reluctance, which related only to the cello part.

"No. Let's do it," he confirmed quickly, praying he could get hold of some strings and find his bow, and that it wasn't wrecked. He'd have no time to break in the strings either.

This was a terrible idea, but he wanted to see Byron, so he was doing it. "I'll text you as soon as I get back."

"On Thursday?"

Pete had meant today, but… "Yeah, and before then—if that's all right? I'd love to know how this evening goes."

"You might regret saying that later."

"I doubt it," Pete said as they moved off again, somehow falling into step with no conscious effort. Byron clicked his key fob as they neared his car.

"Rub an almond on the strings," he said.

"Do what?"

"To help break them in."

"How…?"

"You had a new-strings face."

"That's an actual thing?"

Byron grinned. "Yep. I hope you have a fantastic Christmas."

"Same." Pete didn't make a fool of himself by trying to qualify the way Byron had. He meant it both ways, and there were no guarantees. Sometimes he wondered how they all made it through Christmas alive.

4. Peace on Earth

Byron

CAROLS BY CANDLELIGHT was everything Byron had imagined it would be. As a child, he'd been led to believe Anglican churches were plain and utilitarian compared to their Roman Catholic counterparts, but he'd been inside one or two since and knew better. Even so, St. Mark's C of E was in a class of its own.

All week, people had been gushing about what a huge event this was, so it stood to reason that the outside of the church had been dressed for the occasion. Not in a gaudy, theatrical way. It was still respectful and holy. The trees sparkled gently with white and gold lights, and the building, washed in pale gold, glowed invitingly against the inky sky. A small group of St. Mark's choristers accompanied by a string and wind quartet serenaded the audience…congregation, whichever it was, with traditional carols as they arrived, although by that point, Byron was watching via video screen in the church hall, where the various performers had gathered to get ready.

As for the inside of the church—nothing could have prepared Byron for that.

They'd been in earlier that afternoon for a quick soundcheck, which had been the usual set-up, with techie people running mics and cables, speakers squealing until someone in the know figured out the levels. The overhead lights had been on, and a projector screen hung down in front of the dark chancel, so there was little of interest to see.

Seven o'clock came around, and the video feed switched from exterior to interior view, presenting what appeared to be a black screen. No sound either, and for a moment, Byron panicked on behalf of Reverend Osbourne and everyone else who'd slogged their guts out to put the evening together, but then, from the darkness, came voices, unaccompanied: St. Mark's Church choir singing 'Candlelight' as, one by one, they lit their handheld electronic candles, flickering gold dots shining hope into the bleak of the night.

The carol ended, and the silence resumed, not a single person daring to break it until at last, a spotlight picked out Reverend Osbourne standing over to the left. Byron must've vocalised his surprise, as his head of music chuckled and said quietly, "Scrubs up well, doesn't he?"

Byron nodded. Despite being in the adjacent building, it seemed irreverent somehow to speak, but having seen the reverend in his daytime T-shirts and jeans, 'scrubs up well' was quite the understatement. He *was* wearing a dog collar—beneath a glittery tuxedo—and his hair was smoothed back into a neat ponytail. Very smart and a bit flash, Byron thought, amusing himself momentarily with the notion of their priest donning an outfit like that or anything other than clerical robes. His amusement was short-lived, however, as one of the runners beckoned to the sixth-form ensemble to grab their gear and head over to the church.

So it was that Byron's first proper view of the inside of St. Mark's was leading a bunch of students who were relying on him to keep them calm a when he was completely bowled over by the fit-to-burst pews, with many more people standing at the back of the church. He caught a whiff of those delectable festive smells—mince pies and sherry—and his belly rumbled in anticipation or with nerves, he could no longer tell.

Turning the other way didn't help his disorientation, for there lay the mesmerising magnificence of the chancel.

As Vespers had already taken place, the altar, lectern and pulpit were bedecked not in mournful purple but in celebratory white damask embroidered in gold. To the right was a vast gold-and-white Christmas tree, to the left the choir stalls, dim but for the small circles cast by the reading lights. In front of the altar was an illuminated silhouette Nativity, and both apse stained-glass windows were lit from outside, scattering their colours across the sandstone walls.

"Sir?" one of the sixth formers whispered, drawing him back to the present.

Still overwhelmed, he sat and adjusted his endpin, checked his tuning, decided it would do, and mouthed *ready?* at his fellow musicians. The guitarist rolled his eyes and began strumming the intro to 'Gabriel's Message'. Byron, who wasn't the lead, had been worrying about missing his cue but came in at the right time. With that hurdle out of the way, he found his voice and his confidence, sending up a little thank-you for the wonderful, talented students whose hard work and support for him as well as each other made him feel less like a spotty nerdy kid with no friends and more like Mr. Walker, science teacher, or even Byron 'the new tenor' whom Pete Davenport seemed to like.

He sang so hard his throat ached. All those bits he'd struggled to coordinate bowing and singing during practice flowed without a hitch, and there was a moment when his voice cracked with emotion he had to push down or he'd have cried with the joy of performing one of his favourite Christmas songs at this incredible event. Too soon, his solo was over, although it had never really been *his*, and he joined the congregation in applauding the sixth formers whose performance was worth an A and all the stars in heaven.

With the ensemble piece done, Byron and the students returned to the church hall, where the two sixth formers who were also in the school choir joined their friends: the choir was second to last on the programme.

"Are we OK to go now, Sir?" one of the others asked.

"Yes, of course." Byron couldn't stop smiling. "And well done! You were fantastic!"

The students beamed right back, thanking him for saving the day and wishing him a Merry Christmas before they headed out, guitars on backs, their school work done for the year. They were a great bunch, so talented, and Byron had loved working with them. His common sense was telling him it had to be a one-off. Next year, maybe he'd have time to get more involved. His heart had other ideas, however.

On his way over to check on those who had stayed, he was intercepted by the head of music.

"Hey, I really appreciate you stepping in like that."

"I enjoyed it, Mr. Ashurst."

"I could tell! And call me James, please. It's not easy finding volunteers at this time of year—or willing ones, I should say."

Mr. Ashurst—James—tipped his head toward the gaggle of Moor Croft teachers, all members of the choir, sitting in a circle, some with their phones in their hands, others indulging in low-volume conversation with their neighbours. They all looked like they couldn't wait for it to be over—not a sentiment Byron had ever shared.

"How long have you been singing and playing?" James asked.

"I've been playing since I was four. I had one of those tiny junior cellos about the size of a viola." He'd long outgrown it before his grandad had found a full-sized cello in an antique shop—the one he still played. It was German, built in the 1930s, and that was all he'd been able to find out because there was no maker's name or other features to distinguish it, which was how his grandad had managed to haggle the dealer down to an affordable price. "My mum says I sang before I talked."

James laughed knowingly. "I was the same. So, any chance you're up for doing some extracurricular after Christmas?"

"Definitely." And there went his heart, tromping right through his common sense.

"Smashing! We'll have a meeting sometime first week of Jan and review the timetable, but that's enough talk about work tonight. You know, you can go over to the church and watch if you want."

"Oh! I don't want to leave you short here."

"I'll grab one of that lot if I need to. Go on. You go. I've seen it before."

"OK then, I will!" Byron didn't need telling twice.

Slipping into the foyer at the back of the church, he discovered the source of the decadent festive aroma. Trays of mince pies and glasses of sherry were laid out across several tables being overseen by two older women, who spotted him and beckoned him over.

"You're the one with the lovely voice," said one and handed him a glass of sherry. "Are you old enough to drink?"

"I am. And thank you." Byron accepted the glass and took a small sip. The liquid was warm and soothing in his parched, overworked throat. "I have ID," he said, but the women waved it away.

"Teacher or student?" the other woman asked, offering a mince pie.

"Teacher." Byron politely declined the mince pie. He loved the smell because it reminded him of Christmases with his grandparents, but he wasn't a fan of the taste. "Newly qualified if that makes it any better."

"You're all young to me, lovey."

Byron smiled but didn't comment. Sometimes he didn't feel old or experienced enough to teach A' Level physics, and there were always students who knew more than he did. Perhaps it wasn't that surprising when science had been his second subject. It helped that he'd had a great mentor the previous year, who'd said it was no bad thing to admit to one's limitations.

Students liked showing off their knowledge, and Byron wasn't threatened when they did so, but it was very different from his own experiences as a pupil and in his home life. If he'd ever questioned the how or the why, he'd have been put in his place, so instead he'd complied, which would've been fine if what his parents wanted for him had matched his aspirations.

That was one of the best things about being in a choir or an orchestra, and even being a Christian—the certainty that whatever happened, someone was watching out for him, taking charge when needed, and they were all following the same score. It was also what he tried to provide for his students—a safe space to learn, knowing he wanted their success as much as they did.

Applause from beyond the doors signalled his opportunity to sneak in without disrupting a performance. He quickly glugged the last mouthful of sherry, left his empty glass and thanks with the women and dodged into the church behind those standing in the aisles. The man in front of him was terrific— well over six foot tall with the shoulders of Atlas—and there was a speaker stack to Byron's right, a mixing desk to his left, so he couldn't see a whole lot, but he'd have needed to be in another town to not hear the performing arts students from the local college doing the Trans-Siberian Orchestra's 'Mad Russian's Christmas'. With a full rock band set-up, it was a far cry—and a loud one—from a 'carol by candlelight' and not the sort of thing Byron usually listened to, but he was in awe of their talent. In awe of the whole event.

The big man blocking Byron's view must've been a parent of one of the college band members because he turned and grunted an 'excuse me' as soon as they were done. Byron squashed up against the speaker stack to let him pass but didn't move forward to take his place. The sound was plenty loud enough next to the speakers, never mind in front of them.

After that, he was barely aware of the people around him. He loved live music—as a performer, as an audience member, helping out with the tech stuff, it didn't matter. He rubbed away goosebumps during the mother-daughter duet of 'Mary Did You Know?', awwed along with the parents at a Year Seven group's rendition of 'Twinkle, Twinkle, Little Star/Away in a Manger' and willed strength and positive thoughts to the beginner string players who bravely took on 'What Child is This?' In between times, Reverend Osbourne played the consummate MC, regaling them with terrible Christmas jokes and heart-warming anecdotes.

All too soon, the time came around for Moor Croft High School choir, and as they filed into the church, Byron fought down his sadness that the evening was almost over, refusing to let it destroy his enjoyment of the performance he'd been looking forward to since that first staff meeting, back in September, when Mr. Ashurst had done what was apparently his annual recruitment drive for any musicians on staff who might be willing to offer some of their time and expertise and which Byron had intentionally blocked from his thoughts.

With so little funding for music education, it was the only way most schools could afford to run instrument lessons and extracurricular activities, and it was voluntary, naturally, but that was not the reason it had taken until late November for Byron to come forward. Nor was it really anything to do with his workload as a newly qualified teacher, although it had made a fine excuse.

So he'd been too late to join the choir for Carols by Candlelight, but when St. Mark's Church's spectacular organ struck up the opening fanfare to 'Joy to the World', Byron's regret for not acting sooner fell away like snow off stamped feet when he realised how lucky he was to have this chance to listen and watch his students and colleagues blow the tiles off the roof with their show-stopping song of praise and celebration. Behind the fifty-strong choir, a white light shone down over the chancel, and a shiver of pure wonder raced through Byron's entire being, lifting his spirits and his soul.

Memories of Christmases in what seemed at times a long-distant past came to the fore, of his grandparents picking him up for choir practice and not delivering him back home until they'd had their weekly cup of cocoa, and of Sunday roasts after Mass. He missed them so much, yet this evening, as Moor Croft led the audience into 'O Come All Ye Faithful' followed by 'We Wish You a Merry Christmas', he felt their presence stronger than ever, as if they were standing right there beside him, singing at the tops of their voices. Fourteen years since his grandad went, nine since his gran joined her much-mourned husband; Byron knew now that he would miss them always. The pain of it didn't squeeze his heart so hard these days, but that didn't stop him wishing they were at his side for real.

He wished Pete could've been there too, and when, finally, the last echo of the organ dissipated into the rafters and he, as the one closest to the door, was first to escape the merry warmth of the church, he pulled out his phone, planning his message while he waited for it to start up. *Carols by Candlelight was out of this world! Can't wait for the next one. I miss you.*

He didn't even get as far as opening a new text message. The second his phone picked up a signal, it showed an incoming call from Anna. With a fair idea what his sister had to say and knowing she'd keep calling, he let it go to voicemail while he jogged to his car, answering her third attempt—or sixth, counting those she'd made before he'd turned on his phone.

"Hey, sorry, sis. I was in church."

"Same old excuse. Where are you?"

"In the churchyard now."

"You're supposed to be here, Byron. You *promised*."

"No, actually, I didn't. Mum asked—"

"Mum thinks you're coming tomorrow."

"I told her I wasn't."

"Yeah, but that was in the heat of the moment, wasn't it? You can't *not* come home for Christmas, By. Come on!"

"I'm not coming."

"But he's not here."

"He will be. You know he will."

"The restraining order—"

"Didn't stop him in July. You watch. He'll just turn up for Christmas dinner, acting as if everything's fine, and before you know it, he'll have you believing you chose to study French."

"I *did* choose."

"'Course you did, sis."

"Byron, *please.*"

"No. I'm sorry." It was so hard when he could hear she was in tears, but he'd made the break, and he had to stay strong, stay away, even if it meant spending Christmas on his own, which it did. "Truly, I'm sorry, Anna, but you know I can't. Will you tell Mum I love her?"

"Tell her yourself or go to hell."

"Anna—"

Call ended.

***

Christmas morning Mass was nice, Byron supposed, and well attended, although the church was nowhere near as full as St. Mark's had been. The rest of the choir was in fine spirits—in the physical rather than metaphysical sense in some quarters, mostly the altos—and Byron tried to get in the mood, he really did, but his heart wasn't in it. It must've been obvious too, as every time they came to sing, Norman exchanged hymnals with him, the book already open at the correct page, and mouthed *are you OK?* so often Byron had neck ache from nodding.

He wasn't OK. It was Christmas Day. His mum and sisters had read but not replied to his texts wishing them a Merry Christmas, and he'd stopped trying to call the third time it went unanswered. On top of that, he'd heard nothing at all from Pete since their inaugural number-exchange texts and was at war with himself over it. If they were as alike as Byron thought, Pete would be going through the same debate of whether he should make the first move or take the lack of contact as a sign the other wasn't interested.

It sucked to be an introvert sometimes. Indeed, he was overthinking so much that it was only when Father Benson came to lock up the vestry Byron realised how long he'd been standing there. He hadn't even made it as far as putting on his coat and hastily pulled it around him.

"Sorry, Father. I'll get out of your way."

"No rush, Byron." The priest circled the room, checking the windows were closed and flipping power switches to 'off'. "Looks like you've a lot on your mind."

Byron stayed quiet, not wanting to get into it. The last time he'd spoken to a priest about what had happened was to tell him he'd been duped, like the rest of them, and the priest—the very same man who'd buried his grandparents—had called him a liar. Not to his face. No. He'd popped in on Byron's mum on some pretext or other. Even after she'd corroborated his story, while also making excuses, the priest had still doubted them. Byron wasn't surprised. That was, after all, how gaslighting worked.

Father Benson finished his security circuit and stopped a couple of feet in front of Byron. "I don't know you so well yet, son, and you don't know me, and I may be jumping to conclusions here, but you don't have any family nearby, do you?"

"No, Father, I don't."

"May I ask why you're not with them today?"

"Because…" *He will be there.* "I'm driving home this afternoon." Lying to a priest now. What had he come to?

"All right, well…" The priest moved off, shepherding Byron towards the door. "If it turns out the roads are too icy or for any reason you change your mind, I'd be glad of your company for dinner this afternoon. We'll be sitting down to eat at three. If you're with us, all well and good. If not, I'll know you've gone home and you're not spending the day on your own." He locked the door and fixed Byron with one of those *I can see deep into your soul* gazes. "How does that sound?"

Byron nodded and said, "Thank you, Father." He was grateful for the priest's intervention, but if he couldn't spend the day with his family or Pete, he'd spend it with his cello. "Merry Christmas, Father."

Father Benson sighed, weary and wise. "Merry Christmas, Byron. May the Lord be with you on this day and always."

"And also with your spirit."

5: Dispirited

Pete

HE AND ED hadn't been gone *that* long, but the second they were through the front door, Pete knew they were in trouble. The sounds of boisterous play upstairs heightened the tension of the silence downstairs, and there was nowhere to run, nowhere to hide, so they didn't try. Just kicked off their shoes and strolled into the living room, acknowledged Charlie and Ellie on the sofa, and nonchalantly plonked down in the armchairs as if they'd been there all along.

Charlie sniffed the air. "They serve draught ale in the late shop now, do they?"

"We stopped off for one on the way back," Pete said, shrugging as if it was no biggie. It was all bluster. Ellie was winding up to telling them exactly what she thought of their Boxing Day boozing. Even Charlie, who, as a fellow singleton, was usually on their side, was studying them through narrowed eyes. Then came a loud thump overhead, followed by a child's cry. Pete was probably going to hell for thinking it was a blessing—in fact, he'd appalled himself—but in an instant, their misdemeanour was forgotten as all four siblings sprang to their feet to go to the aid of the injured. Ed was closest to the door and legged it up the stairs, Ellie hot on his heels.

"That sounded like Toby," Pete said, and he was right. By the time he and Charlie reached the stairs, Ellie was on her way back down with her sobbing, snotty-faced son in her arms, an egg growing on his forehead. The cousins trooped behind, trying to tell her what had happened all at the same time.

The explanations became an argument, became a shoving match. Aunty Charlie waded into the throng.

"Come on, monsters." She steered Luke's five-year-old twins, Kali and Kohl, towards the sitting room.

"He just fell, Uncle Pete," Benjamin—Tilly's youngest— repeated a third time. The poor kid was distraught. He was a sensitive soul, nothing like his namesake uncle.

"It's all right, mate. Accidents happen."

The three older cousins came out of the other downstairs room and swept Benjamin into their midst, distracting him with offers of chocolate and racing games. With the crowd dispersed, Ed headed for the toilet and Pete returned to the living room where the twins sat like sulking bookends at either end of the sofa.

"Movie, I reckon," Charlie said, and suddenly they were all enthusiasm, squabbling over the remote control and suggesting films they weren't old enough to watch. Between them, they brought up the listings on the TV and selected *Bend It Like Beckham*. Charlie grabbed the remote control and switched to 'child' mode, muttering to Pete, "How'd they know how to do that?"

He was thinking the same himself, but there'd be no fun in agreeing with her. "You're getting old, sis."

"Pfft. I'm younger than Norman."

Pete laughed and shook his head. "Speaking of, I need to..." Pulling his phone from his pocket, he left the room and dodged out of the front door before anyone could intercept. That pint— OK, those *two pints*—had given him the courage to do what he'd wanted to do for three days, and he needed to act before the effect wore off.

He'd thought Byron might play it cool, but no. He answered on the first ring with a chirpy and surprised-sounding, "Hello!"

"Hey. Happy Boxing Day!"

"And to you. How's it going? Have you had a good Christmas?"

"Yeah, it's been OK, actually. My nephew's just had a little bump on the head, but he's the only casualty so far." Pete searched the vicinity for wood to touch and had to settle for the bare, woody vine of the honeysuckle next to Ben's front door. "How's your Christmas been?"

"Quiet," Byron said. "I've been thinking about the whole cello jam idea."

"Oh?"

"Did I push you into it?"

"No. Well, maybe a bit, but it's about time I did something with the thing, even if I end up selling it. Not that I'm planning to do that, or not yet. I'm totally up for cello jam."

"Are you sure? Only we kind of left it hanging, and I really hope you didn't agree for my sake. I mean, I've been looking forward to playing with you...playing cello with you..." Byron paused, huffed into the phone. "All I'm saying is we don't have to if you don't want. We could just, you know, have a beer, watch a film or something."

"As long as it's not *Bend It Like Beckham*."

"I've not seen that. Is it rubbish?"

"No, it's very good. It's about a female footballer, and it's my sister's favourite film, but I've seen it so many times I know most of the lines."

"Do you follow football?"

"Not really. My sister Charlie's a coach and played for England when she was younger, so I used to watch her games."

"Wait—did you say she played for England? That's amazing!"

"It is." Pete sometimes overlooked how impressive that sounded to other people since Charlie's career had begun when he was still potty-training, which wasn't to say his family was unaware of her talent, but it was part of their normal. "Are you a footy fan?" he asked, hoping the answer was no, although if it was yes, he was sure he could get interested pretty darn quickly.

"I'm afraid not. The only thing I know about football is there are eleven players on each side."

"Unless it's five-a-side."

Byron laughed. "Good point."

"Anyway, enough about footy," Pete said. "In answer to your question, yes, I'm sure. Cello, film—I don't mind, although I got my cello down before we left on Sunday, and I've ordered new strings, so let's do this thing. Did we say Friday?"

"We did. What time? After lunch?"

"Works for me. Text me your address."

"Will do."

"Great." Pete vented a breath. He was feeling 100% sober now and 200% relieved Byron still wanted to get together. He only wished he hadn't put off calling for so long. "What did you get for Christmas?"

"Oh, nothing exciting. You?"

"A remote-control drone." Pete took a step back as he said it and glanced up on the off chance it had all been a dream. Sadly not. "I attempted to fly it through my brother's bedroom window without opening it first."

"Oops!"

"Yeah. He wasn't best pleased. We do a Secret Santa so we don't all end up with a shed load of presents, and he doesn't know who to blame. Speak of the devil…"

The front door opened, and Ben poked his head out, frowning. "Who's that you're talking to?"

"Nobody you know."

"Suit yourself. We're getting out the board games." Ben shut the door again.

"Awesome," Pete muttered. Just one of the many reasons he hated coming here every year—the expectation they'd all comply and do whatever Ben dictated. In the end, resistance was futile, or at least, it wasn't worth the hassle. "I'd better go, Byron, even though I'd much rather talk to you."

"We can talk again later. If you want to."

"Yeah, I really do."

"OK. I'll send that text now, give you a call later and see you the day after tomorrow!"

"Perfect." They said their goodbyes and Pete returned inside, fighting to shift the smile off his face. Monopoly or Scrabble or whatever 'delight' his brother thrust on them no longer felt such a trial.

* * *

Two a.m. was way too late and Pete was far too drunk to type a text message. They did this thing on Boxing Day, which had started life as a basic buffet to get rid of leftovers but over the years, and in tandem with Ben pimping up his crib, had become a family extravaganza of Fun! and Games! If Pete was honest, he did kind of enjoy it, despite his siblings' competitiveness turning everything into a contest. DDR, Guitar Hero, karaoke, foosball, air hockey, pool—the rules were the same. They drew names for the opening heats and played knockouts until there was a winner, however long it took, for there could be only one.

And so it came to pass that Tilly and their dad, by sheer luck and with not a shred of pool talent between them, had laughed and cried their way through the final for the past *two hours*! Why had Pete decided that was a golden opportunity to match his dad, shot for shot, on the Irish whiskey? Because drinking himself under the table had seemed infinitely preferable to watching pool balls ping off the cushions, except for the white, of course. That one had no trouble finding the pockets.

Are you awake?

"Noooo!" Pete stared at his thumb, aghast, as it became two thumbs, which did a little jig, looking very pleased with themselves, before coalescing into one treacherous, send-pressing digit. "Why you do that, idiot?" Too late now.

Yes.

"Oh!" Pete squinted at the tiny text at the top of the screen even though he knew what it said. "Byron is typing," he read aloud.

Calling you.

"Byron is calling." And so he was, but in his drunken haste to accept, Pete dropped his phone, and with a greedy gulp, the duvet swallowed it. "Where the…" Pete patted and poked and shook it down and threw the blasted thing on the floor. No phone. It was lost forever.

***

"…you need to get a wiggle—why are you on the floor?"

"Go away." The rug was gritty and stank of fake lavender, but Pete didn't dare move in case his head actually did split in half.

"Oh!" Charlie laughed, sober and merciless. "I had a feeling you were hammered."

"Leave me alone."

"No can do, matey. If you're coming back with me, you need to be ready in half an hour."

"Time is it?"

"Nine or thereabouts. I'm going to the match this afternoon, remember?"

He didn't remember. "OK. I'm getting up." He lifted his head—"Ugh"—and put it down again, deciding 'up' was a bit ambitious. He attempted a roll instead. Success!

"Oh, lordy," Charlie said, and she sounded serious.

"What?"

"I think you might be allergic to Jameson's."

Now she'd mentioned it, he *was* feeling a bit wheezy, but he'd drunk whiskey before. Admittedly, not half a bottle, but still. He'd have noticed if he'd reacted to it, so it had to be something else. Something like…

"Shake n' Vac."

"You're kidding me." Charlie was already rooting through Pete's bag for his inhaler and pills. "I'm gonna kill Ben."

"Not his fault." Pete shuffled back until he was sitting against the wall. "He didn't know I was going to crash out on the floor."

"But he knows he can't use that stuff when you're here." She handed over his inhaler.

"Thanks." Pete shook it and took a dose. "Maybe we went too far insulting his hospitality this time and he's picking us off one by one."

"Joke all you like. You haven't seen your face yet. Say cheese." She held up her phone, catching him mid-second dose of inhaler, and showed him the photo.

"Oh my God." Now he could see it, the rash started to itch. He snagged the antihistamines and with much effort swallowed one. "Charlie, what am I gonna do? This is awful!"

"Do we need to go to A and E?"

"I mean I'm seeing Byron tomorrow. Oh…" And now he remembered the drunk text. "Can you see my phone anywhere? I need to call him."

She flipped a pillow and found it straight away. "Priorities and all that, dude."

"I haven't had a date in two years, *dude*."

"Yeah, well, they're like buses, aren't they?"

"For you, they are," Pete grumbled bitterly and snatched the phone from her.

"You'll be fine by tomorrow. Come on. Get up, get a shower. You smell like the Irish club after the cleaner's been in." Charlie headed for the door.

"Yeah, thanks for that."

"Welcome," she said and left him to make his apologies to Byron, shower and figure out what to do about his face.

***

Pete couldn't restring a cello to save his life. He wasn't sure he'd ever tried before, but he persevered until he snapped a second string—it was as well he'd ordered two sets—at which point he shoved his cello across the bed in disgust. The solitary attached string gave a twang of protest and unravelled from its peg.

"See if I care," he muttered. He turned his back on it and picked up his phone. He was in half a mind to cancel anyway. He'd accepted he was going to make a show of himself, seeing as he couldn't get his instrument into good enough shape to practise and he'd barely made it to Grade 5 standard—enough for high school orchestra and GCSE Music. Much as he wanted to make a good impression, he wouldn't be doing so with his musical prowess, and that was OK. But what else did he have to offer? A career in recycling? His good looks? Hardly.

Unsightly as it was, the rash on his face wasn't anywhere near as itchy as it had been yesterday, especially on the way home from Ben's, when Charlie had threatened to throw him out on the motorway if he elbowed her one more time. He'd sat on his hands the rest of the way home and then slathered hydrocortisone cream over pretty much his entire head.

So it was no longer itchy, but a quick diagnostic selfie confirmed his left cheek and the left side of his forehead and nose were a flaky disaster, and his Mr. Potato Head lips were stuck in a numb pout like he was angling for a kiss no-one in their right mind would deliver.

Maybe Byron didn't wear his glasses at home and wouldn't notice. But then he'd have to put them on to read music.

The music Pete couldn't play.

He brought up Byron's number.

"Hey."

"Hey, Pete. I was just…"

Pete grimaced as Byron's cheerfulness plummeted faster than a diving submarine. Of course he'd have figured out why

Pete was calling an hour before they were supposed to meet. It was a horrible experience, getting the blow-off, and a horrible thing to do to someone. Pete didn't want to be that guy, not least because now he'd heard Byron's voice, he absolutely didn't want to cancel.

"You were just...?" he prompted.

"Icing faces onto gingerbread men."

"That's...not what I was expecting!" Pete laughed and heard Byron's relief as he joined in. "Don't suppose you gave any of them super-fat lips?"

"They have different-coloured buttons if that helps?"

"It might," Pete said. "I've got this rash on my face. Well, on half my face. I need a Phantom of the Opera mask."

"Oh, no! What's that from?"

"I passed out, didn't I?"

"Yeah?"

"On the rug, and it was full of carpet freshener."

"Ah. So did you want to postpone today?"

"I was going to, but no, I still want to come. Just try not to laugh, OK?"

"I won't laugh. I promise."

"Maybe not at my face, but..." Pete reached behind him and plucked the saggy cello string, which obliged with a dull *boing*.

"Is that what I think it is?"

"A one-stringed, very dusty cello? Yeah, I might need your assistance."

Byron chuckled. "You have it. See you in a little while."

"You will. And thank you."

"That's what friends are for, isn't it?"

"It is," Pete said. *Friends. OK.* He could go with that.

6: Epiphany

Byron

SWEEPING THE SNOWDRIFT of icing sugar from the kitchen counter, Byron shushed the tiny shoulder devil telling him he'd gone overboard, though he couldn't deny it when the evidence was all around him—a dozen smiling gingerbread men; a frosted chocolate yule log; the party platter in the freezer— and that was just the kitchen. In the living room, there was a six-foot, pre-lit tree; holly garlands adorned the banister, and lights twinkled around every window. In his defence, he'd hit the Boxing Day sales and acquired the decorations for a song—well, he'd had to part with a bit of cash too—then spent a day and a half decorating his tiny house and baking up a storm.

Had he done it purely to hide that he'd spent Christmas alone? He desperately hoped not. Even with the best of intentions, like making it so Pete wouldn't feel bad for enjoying time with his family, a relationship built on lies caused a world of pain for everyone. Maybe Byron was getting ahead of himself in thinking what they had *was* the beginning of something special, but if it was, he wanted to start on the right foot.

It certainly felt different from his previous relationships in a way he couldn't define, other than knowing he didn't want to put on an act as they explored whatever this was. Equally, he wasn't sure he was ready to share the full sorry saga yet and took some solace from being able to truthfully say he'd been too busy with school work to decorate the house before Christmas.

With the chocolate yule log finished and stowed in a cake box, he had a last check around. There was plenty of beer, pop and juice in the fridge. The lights were on or off, depending on whether they were festive or functional. Nothing had spilt down his clothes. That done, he carried the kitchen stool through to the living room and put it next to his cellist chair. His music and cello were already in there.

When he'd moved in, he'd set up his desk and computer in the smaller bedroom, and he did use it for work, but he couldn't practise up there. All his life, he'd been told music was 'just a hobby'. Intrinsically, he knew that was false, but it made no difference. It still felt wrong doing it in a designated workspace or during the workday.

Besides, the cello and wooden music stand made for an eye-catching feature in his otherwise bare-basics living room. One day, he'd get around to buying some brightly coloured cushions and hang a couple of pictures on the walls. For now, the plain, black sofa, tiny square table and average-sized TV met his needs, and it was easy to keep clean, but that didn't stop him triple-checking all was shipshape when the letterbox flapped at one minute to two.

Byron was grinning as he opened the door. "You're just in time!"

"Ha, yeah. That's me," Pete said drolly. "My line manager calls me that. It took me ages to figure out why."

"Um…you've lost me," Byron admitted, sweeping his arm in a *mi casa es tu casa* gesture.

"Justin Time," Pete explained. "Apparently, it's frowned upon to come screeching up to deadlines. I think she'd prefer I missed them entirely." He stepped in, rested his cello case against the wall and then, quite unexpectedly, hugged Byron and kissed his cheek. "Belated Merry Christmas, Mr. Walker."

Bashful and surprised, but in the best possible way, Byron shut the door and joked, "Is that a Hallmark movie?"

Pete laughed. "It could be, couldn't it? Wow." He stopped halfway along the hall, next to the living room door, and openly surveyed his surroundings. "What a great place!"

"Thanks. I bought it through a shared ownership scheme for new teachers, so it's a bit of a work in progress. It needs...I don't know. Personalising, I guess. It still feels like I'm renting, if you see what I mean."

"Yeah, I do." Pete unfastened his scarf—a Christmas acquisition, gauging by its fluffiness—but kept it on, the dangling ends forming charcoal chenille stage curtains to the singing tree on his sweatshirt. Pete noticed Byron looking at it. "The mandatory ugly Christmas jumper."

"I like it."

"Me too," Pete said, casting an eye over Byron's very un-festive blue grandad shirt and jeans. "Where's yours?"

"I don't have one."

"Well, we'll have to do something about that next Christmas. To be fair, this is better than I usually get. It's always something to do with trees—who'd be an environmental scientist, eh?" Pete carried on while Byron was still caught on *next Christmas*. It had tripped off Pete's tongue so naturally, as if it were a given they'd still be friends a year from now.

"Byron? Are you OK?"

"Um...yes. Sorry." The bokeh of the twinkle lights came back into focus. "Too early for a beer?"

Pete grinned. "It's *never* too early for a beer."

Byron led the way into the kitchen, where he took a couple of cans from the fridge and handed one to Pete. "I wasn't sure if you'd want to wait until after we'd practised."

"It ain't gonna make me play any worse. Cheers." A hiss of gas escaped the top of Pete's can as he opened it and took a generous swig. It was only as he put his head back, exposing more of his chin and neck, that Byron—he may have been ogling—noticed the rash, followed by the blush as Pete lowered the can and self-consciously pulled up his scarf.

"It's not that bad," Byron said. "Or not to look at. Is it itchy?"

"On and off. My lips still feel weird, though. Heh. It's a shame I don't play a wind instrument. At least I'd have an excuse for being crap."

Byron made himself stop trying to see if Pete's lips *looked* weird—they didn't—and thumbed over his shoulder. "We should probably get those strings sorted so you can show me exactly how crap you are."

"I suppose," Pete mumbled but headed back to the hall and picked up his cello case, waiting for Byron to invite him in before he entered the living room. His eyes widened when he saw Byron's cello in the corner. "That's beautiful."

"Thanks. My grandad bought it ready for when I moved up from three-quarter size. It's not a well-known make, but I love the way it sounds and feels. I guess that's mostly sentimental. My grandad never got to hear me play it—he died when I was eleven, my gran when I was sixteen, and I really miss them, but when I sing or play, I know they're still with me."

The warmth of Pete's smile as he listened stopped Byron from fleeing to the bathroom for a good old cry. He'd never told anyone that before and was choking up a bit but managed to quip, "I've shown you mine…" and redirected to the canvas case in Pete's hands.

"Right, yeah. Mine's a cheap one. Or cheapish. My mum still likes to tell me they missed out on a trip to Florida to pay for it." He set the case on the floor, undid the zip and flipped it open. "Da-dah!"

"Looks decent," Byron said.

"You know what they say about a bad workman blaming his tools?"

"You're front-loading then. Gotcha." It had occurred to Byron that Pete might be laying it on, insisting he was awful when he was actually brilliant, but he seemed genuinely nervous. That was so far away from what Byron had intended for their afternoon, he had to do something before it was too late.

"Listen, Pete. I know I said it already, but we really don't have to do this. I'm just happy you're here and we get to spend some time together away from…"

"Norman?" Pete suggested.

"I was going to say the choir as a whole. Norman seems OK mostly. Am I missing something?"

"No. He is OK. A really nice fella."

There was a 'but' in that statement; Byron decided to wait rather than prompt, and it was a good thing he was both quite a patient person and distracted by Pete bending over his cello case. He'd always thought Pete had a nice bum, but it was usually either hidden by his alb or being sat upon. Now, as he knelt on the floor, it rested on his heels and tensed when Pete twisted towards Byron, offering the new strings.

"Help?" he said with a ghost of a cheeky smirk that Byron wanted so much to kiss but settled for brushing his fingers against Pete's as he took the strings from him. He hated being so shy when it came to affection and intimacy. It was especially frustrating when he had the confidence to stand in front of thirty-plus students every day and sing solos before hundreds of people yet couldn't articulate his growing feelings for Pete.

He'd realised during his preparations that it had nothing to do with his competency as a musician or a scientist, nor his fears of inadequacy as a friend or, dare he think it, a boyfriend. It was about having an audience of one, and his frequent offers to ditch cello duets in favour of watching a film were as much for his sake as Pete's.

Glad for the excuse to put it off a bit longer, Byron knelt beside Pete and took his cello, turning it from side to side, feeling its weight. On closer inspection, it wasn't too shabby in make or state of repair, with only a few surface scratches, and the bridge was slightly warped but playable. Byron worked in silence, making sure Pete could see as he intently followed along.

"It'll take a day or two for them to settle," Byron said once all four strings were in place and tuned. "You'll probably need to retune it more than usual."

"Once every couple of years, then," Pete joked, staring at the instrument as if it might at any given moment turn into a cobra and strike a deadly blow. "Thanks."

"Anytime. You know, before Carols by Candlelight, I hadn't played in front of anyone for five years."

"But you still practised every day, I bet."

Byron nodded. "It's not the same as rehearsing with other people, though. I miss it."

"In that case…" Lightly squeezing Byron's shoulder, Pete got up, collected his cello and bow and went to look at the music on the stand. "What are we playing?" He frowned as he studied the notation, then flipped to the book's cover. "Ah—2Cellos. These guys are really good." Whether he was conscious of it, Byron couldn't tell, but Pete's fingers moved over the strings for a moment before he said, "I think I can manage that."

"Have my chair," Byron offered, but Pete was already sitting on the kitchen stool and adjusting his endpin.

"This isn't going to wreck the rug, is it?"

"That's what it's there for."

With a couple of adjustments, Pete assumed a playing position. It came naturally, born of muscle memory, indicating that even if he didn't play regularly now, he had in the past. He bowed across the strings, testing the tuning, and played a slightly disjointed C major scale, two octaves up and down.

"I'm gonna pay for this tomorrow," he said, rotating his shoulder, then glancing over it at Byron. "So are you, if you don't get your backside over here ASAP."

Byron sighed out a reluctant, "OK," then paused halfway across the room to clean his glasses on his shirt, having suddenly noticed they were dusty with icing sugar. *Procrastinating.* That was what he was doing. He'd learnt during his teacher training that students did it when they were afraid the task they had to complete would worsen their situation—destroy their good mood or lead to failure—and that made a lot of sense. As things stood, he and Pete had a good, solid friendship; what they were about to do could ruin everything.

Pete was sawing his way through 'With or Without You'—fittingly ironic—and his playing lacked confidence, but he *was* playing. He'd said he'd wanted to do this, which gave Byron two options: he could keep on worrying that he'd manipulated Pete into *thinking* he wanted it, or he could trust Pete—and himself. Either way, he was going over there right now, picking up his cello and playing.

Of course, it wasn't *quite* that easy, as Byron's living room was small, and he had to shimmy past the Christmas tree and limbo under Pete's bowing arm to reach his chair. He'd changed his strings prior to Carols by Candlelight and would've liked to tune up, but he didn't want to interrupt Pete. There was something romantic about joining in rather than starting over, of one becoming two, becoming one.

As Pete reached the second chorus, Byron joined him, matching his tempo. It wasn't perfect. Their tuning was definitely off, and their attacks and releases needed work. Still, a tingle tickled down Byron's back, building into a full-body shiver as they hit the last note, dimmed and cut off together.

"Amazing!" Pete turned toward Byron, both of them smiling. "I've got goosebumps!"

"Me too."

"You're so good."

"Thanks. You're pretty good yourself."

"I was better than I thought I'd be. Will you play something for me?"

"Solo, you mean?"

"Yeah."

"I will, but don't you want to play something else?"

"After you've performed for me." Pete turned his cello so it rested against one knee and sat back expectantly. And because Byron was high on adrenaline, he obliged. He didn't pick anything showy, opting for 'I Heard the Bells on Christmas Day'—the more syncopated version, not the staid carol they sang at Mass. He loved the intervals and the long notes, and how the crescendo sent the melody soaring heavenwards for the final, hopeful verse.

Only when he stopped playing did Byron realise he'd had his eyes closed, and he opened them to Pete's overt admiration.

"That was so beautiful, Byron."

"I'm pleased you enjoyed it. It was my gran's favourite. It used to make her cry."

"It is very moving," Pete agreed. "How long have you been playing, really?"

"Since I was four."

"What are you? Grade 8?"

Byron nodded. "For what it's worth. So what shall we play next?" He flipped through the book on the stand. "I've got a book of Christmas carols if you'd prefer." Anything to avoid Pete asking more questions.

"I don't mind," Pete said. "Slow and easy's good."

"I'll go and see what else I have in my office." Setting his cello back on its stand, Byron left the room, dilly-dallying in the hallway. Should he invite Pete to come with him? Would it send too strong a signal? It wasn't the *wrong* signal, but if a romantic relationship was in their future, they were a long way off taking it to the bedroom. It didn't have to mean anything—Pete would have to go upstairs if he needed to use the bathroom anyway. Still, it seemed too forward to say, "Want to come up and see my collection of music scores?"

Frustrated by once again overthinking what *would have* been an innocent question, had he the gall to ask it, Byron ran up to his office and retrieved the entire box of scores, returned downstairs and set it on the floor in front of the music stand.

"Another beer?"

"Please." Pete passed up his empty can and gestured to the box. "Mind if I take a look?"

"Be my guest."

Byron left again, smiling at Pete's monologue of, "God, no," followed by a rustle of paper, then, "What the...?" He sang a few notes, said, "Nope. No— Oh!" Silence. It lasted maybe five seconds—just long enough for Byron to predict with 100% accuracy what came next.

Bah-da, bah-da, bah-da da-da-da, bah-da, bah-da, bah-da da-da-da—the intro bars to 'He's a Pirate', technically tricky in places, but Pete knew the tune, and that was a sure-fire way to get even a novice playing a complex piece without hesitating or second-guessing themselves, not that Pete was a novice by any stretch. However, sight-reading took practice, and by his own admission, he hadn't ever been big on that so relied on playing by ear. Very nice ear. Both of them. And the rest of him. Byron sighed deeply, sending his whispered wish ahead of him. *Please make the first move.*

If there were ever a chance of a wish being heard, it would need to be made in a much quieter place than Byron's living room. He lingered in the doorway, entranced by Pete's loud, confident bowing. Whether he was aware he had an audience, Byron couldn't tell—until Pete pulled out of the last note and turned, exhilarated and grinning as if he'd disembarked from a roller coaster.

"I really missed this!"

Byron laughed. "I can tell."

"I'm totally in the zone now." Setting aside his cello, Pete scooped half the scores from the box and started sorting them, propping some on the stand and moving the others to the back of the pile on his lap. He was so absorbed in his task, Byron didn't bother offering him the beer and instead left the cans on the table before resuming his seat alongside Pete.

Those beers went warm long before they got around to drinking them. They attempted every duet in Byron's collection. Some were far from note-perfect, but perfection wasn't important. They laughed through their mistakes, shared memories connected to each piece, agreeing that at some point they'd watch *Titanic* together, given they'd played 'My Heart Will Go On' without so much as looking at the printed score and could quote entire scenes even though neither of them had ever seen the film.

"And we should do this again," Pete said as he put his cello away just before seven. "Soon."

"Tomorrow?" Byron kept his tone light so it could be taken as a joke or a hopeful suggestion.

"I'd love to, but I'm working until five. Is that too late?"

"Not for me."

"Not for me either." Pete's phone vibrated, and he checked the screen. "That's Charlie outside." He bent to pick up his cello.

"You can leave that here if you want," Byron offered.

"It won't be in your way?"

"I'll pop it behind the stand. It'll be fine." And there he went again, second-guessing his intent—kindness or a way to guarantee Pete came back?

"Brilliant." Pete retrieved his scarf from the back of the sofa and looped it around his neck, once again leaving the ends dangling. Byron was struck by a fierce urge to grab those ends and tug Pete to him. It was so vivid, he felt the soft chenille in his hands, Pete's soft lips on his, and for a moment believed he'd acted upon it. He hadn't, and the mess of frustration and relief stayed with him long after Pete had gone home.

7: Those Who Can

Pete

IT TOOK ONLY two jamming sessions for Pete to accept that Byron was leagues beyond him on the cello, although, humble soul that he was, Byron kept up the façade of praise, and Pete might even have believed it if Charlie hadn't brought him back to earth with a bump.

"Whatcha watching? Porn?" she asked even though he was sitting at the kitchen table and their parents were in the room next door.

"Must be some high-class porn you watch if it has a classical music soundtrack."

"Dude, there's nothing classical about that racket." She looked over his shoulder, digging her chin in until he side-butted her. "Who's play— Oh. Ohhhhh…it's you and Norman." Charlie moved away—thank goodness; she had a very heavy, pointy chin—and filled the kettle.

"Byron," Pete corrected wearily. The joke was wearing thin.

"Now *he's* good."

Pete ignored the implicit criticism. "He is. He's *really* good. Like, should be in a symphony orchestra good."

"Well, he is a music teacher, isn't he?"

"Nope."

"I swear you told me he taught at Moor Croft."

"I did, and he does. Science."

"OK." She lined up four mugs and dropped a teabag into each. "Sounds like wasted talent to me."

"Yeah, tell me about it," Pete agreed vaguely, thinking back to Byron's non-explanation for why he'd chosen to study physics at uni when he'd been offered a place at the Royal Conservatoire. His exact words: "Those who can, do." The old cliché, except he *could*, but he *hadn't*, and what's more, he'd given off a clear *please don't ask me to explain* vibe, so Pete had done what he *could do* as a good friend. He'd let it go.

"So is it official yet?" Charlie deposited two mugs on the table and plonked down in the chair next to his. Pete locked his phone and put it away.

"Where's Mum and Dad's tea?"

"I just took it in to them."

"Did you?"

"Blimey, you've got it bad."

"Shut up. We're just friends."

"Yeah, right."

"Even if I wanted more, school starts back on Thursday, and he's got all that newly qualified teacher stuff to deal with, hasn't he?" Never mind that Byron didn't seem interested in anything more than friendship.

"But you really like him," Charlie said. It wasn't a question.

"Yeah, I do."

"And he really likes you."

Pete shrugged.

"He's mega busy with work, yet he's still managed to carve out time to spend with you this weekend."

"Maybe I'm his default timeout? He doesn't really have any other friends here."

"Default timeout? Whatever."

"What's that supposed to mean?"

Charlie shook her head, laughing at him. "Think about it. You're both tenors in the church choir, both play cello—"

"Arguable."

"Both have a science background. You're the same age. You literally couldn't have more in common."

"Yeah, but *opposites* attract. Isn't that what they say?"

"Since when were you such a pessimist?"

"Since David moved out."

"That was three years ago. And you've been with other people."

He had, it was true, but they were one-offs—a couple of drinks, an agreement they'd text, and done. "It's different this time," he said.

"Yeah, I'm getting that." Charlie stood, tea in hand. "I've got car videos to edit and upload. You wanna help?"

"Ha, no."

"Fair enough. I'll be in my room if you need me, OK?"

"Why would I—"

She lightly cuffed his ear. "In a bit."

"Yeah," Pete said, calling, "Thanks, Charlie," when she was halfway up the stairs. She gave him a thumbs-up over the banister.

She was right, though. The previous evening at Byron's, when Pete had gone up to use the bathroom, he'd caught a glimpse of the study through the open door. The desk was stacked with students' exercise books and project folders, and there was an enormous ring binder on the floor, fluorescent tabs marking various pages, too many to count. The computer monitor displayed three open documents, and presumably there was a noticeboard behind all those papers pinned above the desk. Yet Byron had invited him over two days in a row; adding in Mass this morning, they'd seen each other every day since Pete got back from Ben's.

That wasn't enough to stop Pete from coming up with excuses to see Byron again tomorrow. If anything, it was having the opposite effect—he just couldn't seem to get enough. But perhaps that was because Byron wasn't giving him enough.

Sure, they'd spent a lot of time together. They'd played duets for hours, and Byron had retuned Pete's cello whenever it needed it. Pete had told Byron all about Christmas at Ben's and how every year there was some big bust-up or other. He'd told him about the non-date with Norman and about David too, mainly to fill the awkward silence that ensued from asking how Byron's family celebrated Christmas. They'd drunk beer and then more beer and watched *Titanic*—it was almost two a.m. before they were done sharing their favourite bits and fact-checking whether the musicians really had played as the ship sank. Apparently so.

"Have you had another accident with the Airfix glue, Peter?" his dad tormented, ruffling Pete's hair as he passed behind his chair. Pete chuckled and picked up his tea; it was lukewarm, confirming he'd been sitting there, lost in thought, for quite some time.

"I'll come in now. What are you and Mum watching?"

"Not a clue. It's just on. Your mum's doing that needlework thing, and I've got that flaming jigsaw, haven't I? If you want to give me a hand with that, you're welcome."

"Yeah, I might do, actually. Shall I make more tea?"

"No, you're all right. We're having a *drink* drink. Want a beer?"

"Why not? It's Christmas, isn't it? Sort of."

"Sort of's good enough." Groaning, his dad reached up into the cupboard and retrieved a whiskey tumbler and sherry schooner, his face scrunched with the pain he liked to pretend he didn't have.

"You go sit, Dad. I'll bring in the drinks." Acting decisively to save argument, Pete collected the Jameson's, Harvey's and a bottle of beer and followed his dad into the living room, where a historical drama was playing to itself and his mum was frowning at a square of white fabric. She peered over the top of her glasses at him.

"I thought you'd gone out."

"Nope." He deposited the sherry bottle on her chair-side table and took the schooner from his dad. "Want me to pour it?"

"What d'you bring the bottle in for?" his mum complained. "I'll only drink it."

"That's what it's for, love," his dad said and, with more groaning, eased back into his spot at the other end of the sofa. Once he was settled, Pete handed him the Jameson's, having discreetly loosened the cap first, and sat on the floor beside the coffee table, its entire surface scattered with jigsaw pieces.

"How long have you been at this?" he asked.

"Not long," his dad said. His mum made a *pfft* sound.

"You haven't even sorted out the edge pieces."

"That's because it doesn't have any. Here." His dad kicked the box across the floor. Pete flipped it over and started to laugh.

"No way!" It was a 3D puzzle of the *RMS Titanic*. "We watched this last night."

"Grand film, that."

"It is," his mum agreed. "Who's 'we'? You and the new tenor?"

"Yeah."

"I wondered why you were home so late."

"Now then, Marie," his dad warned.

"What? I mean it's a long film!"

Pete's dad shook his head and poured a healthy measure of whiskey into his glass. "How did you get on with your cello?"

"Fine." He shuffled the pieces around and spotted a bunch that were mostly red—the keel. That seemed as good a place to start as any.

"Did you actually play it?" his mum asked.

"I did. For about ten hours."

"Blimey. He's a good influence."

Pete kept his mouth shut and carried on sorting pieces.

"So he's not from around here then?"

"Nope."

"And what about his mum and dad?"

"Dunno. He doesn't talk about them."

"Oh." His mum went back to scowling at her fabric, every so often casting suspicious glances Pete's way, as if he were being deliberately obtuse. From what Byron had said, he'd been very close to his grandparents, who were both dead. Otherwise, the only thing he'd shared about his family was that one sister was at uni and the other had married a Protestant—before turning the conversation back on Pete, which was how it had gone every time. For whatever reason, Byron didn't like talking about himself, be that his family or his music, and so Pete had stopped probing. He wanted to get to know Byron, but he also respected Byron's privacy.

"Surely he spent Christmas with them."

"Not everyone spends Christmas with their family, Mum."

"Yes, well, your dad and I had a chat about that, didn't we, love?"

"That we did."

"Maybe it's time you flew the nest—"

"Wait! You're kicking me out?"

"No, you daft beggar. Like we told you when you came home from university, you're always welcome here, for as long or as often as you need. But I think maybe you and your sister have outgrown Christmas."

"Charlie…" Pete braced, ready to march upstairs and strangle her if she'd dropped him in it. "What did she say?"

"*Charlotte* didn't say anything. Matilda did."

"She's such a tattler."

"Oh, Peter, don't be like that. She's got a sensible head on her shoulders, that girl."

"That's not what you said when she got preg—"

"Peter!" That was his dad this time, and Pete bowed his head, contrite.

"Sorry, Mum."

She flared her nostrils and continued, "All I'm saying is you shouldn't feel obliged to spend Christmas with us."

"I don't."

"But if you did—"

"I don't!" He had no idea why he was arguing when that was exactly how he—and Charlie—felt. Obliged. He should have been elated at being cut loose; instead, his heart sank faster than those heroic musicians aboard the *Titanic*. Of course, his mother wasn't above playing mind games to secure her children's compliance. Reverse psychology, she called it, and it worked, given she'd brought up seven and never raised a hand to any of them.

"There's no need to decide anything now, sweetie. It's a year away, after all. But if you and Byron have other things you'd rather be doing at Christmas, then you should do them, build your own traditions."

"Er..." This conversation had taken a very unexpected and not entirely comfortable turn. "We're just friends, Mum."

"Like you and David were just housemates?"

"No. Well..." *Damn.* He'd fallen right into that one. "We really are only friends—at the moment."

"Then let's wait and see, shall we? Now..." She set aside the fabric square and picked up her sherry. "What are your plans for tomorrow? I hope you're taking him somewhere nice."

"I haven't asked him." *Yet.* But he was going to, just as soon as he'd figured out how to escape this surreal evening with his parents.

***

Options. He needed some, and on 30th December, finding anywhere that still had tickets available for New Year's Eve would constitute the second miracle of the day. Still, Pete sent up a prayer as he dialled the jazz bar's number. It was engaged. He hung up, counted to thirty and tried again. It rang out.

"Rhythm and Booze."

"Hi there. I wondered if you had two tickets available for tomorrow evening."

"As luck would have it, someone just cancelled two reservations. They're yours if you want them."

"I do." Pete mouthed *thank you*. "Should I come down and collect them, or…?"

"Can you pay by card?"

"Yep. Sure."

"Then I'll take your payment and your details over the phone, and you can pick them up on arrival."

"Perfect." Pete dug out his wallet and went through the payment process, baulking slightly at the cost. There was no guarantee Byron would accept his invitation, but he couldn't afford to wait. If it came to it, he could always go on his own. Or ask Norman. Or not.

"That's all gone through for you. To confirm: two tickets in the name of Pete Davenport for the New Year's Eve party."

"Yes."

"Great. See you tomorrow."

"Thanks. Bye." Pete flopped back on his bed and took a moment to catch his breath. His heart was thumping so hard his T-shirt shifted with each beat. He'd never done anything so forward in his life, and it was terrifying, although Byron had accepted his hugs and cheek kisses and hadn't mocked his awful playing. Whether it was friendship or more, they had *something*—enough that Pete trusted Byron to let him down gently if he didn't want to or couldn't spend New Year's Eve with him. He'd find out soon enough.

"Hey, it's me."

"Hey. Hang on." The background music at Byron's end of the line stopped. "Sorry. I was listening to Apocalyptica."

"They're a rock band, right?"

"That's right. A cello rock band."

"Oh, cool. I'll have to give them a listen. How's your Sunday been?"

"Kind of quiet. I was going to ring you earlier, but...well, YouTube."

Pete laughed. It was a relief to know he wasn't the only one who'd been wanting to call. "So, you like rock music, but how do you feel about jazz?"

"It's music. I love it all."

"Even that weird minimalist stuff we studied for GCSE?"

"OK, maybe not quite *all*. Why d'you ask?"

"Well...so...the thing is...do you know there's a jazz club on the high street?"

"Yes. I've driven past it a few times. What's it like?"

"Great atmosphere. Amazing music. Decent beer."

"Sounds like my kind of place."

"I'm glad you said that because I wondered if you'd consider going there with me tomorrow evening."

"Oh, Pete, I really would love to, but I need to be somewhere in the afternoon. What time were you thinking?"

"Their website says from eight till two. It's OK if you can't make it."

"Are you going with other people?"

There was no getting around answering that without blatantly lying or throwing a guilt trip Byron's way, and while Pete fumbled for an excuse, Byron hummed in thought.

"What if I could be there for ten? Would that work?"

"Totally, but—"

"No buts. I can't promise anything, other than an explanation. I owe you that much. I will try my absolute best to get there for ten."

"I'll have a beer waiting for you."

"Thank you." Byron's shaky sigh was loud in Pete's ear but impossible to interpret.

"I'll see you tomorrow, By."

"That's what my sisters call me. See you tomorrow, and thank you again."

"No, thank *you* for saying yes." Pete took a chance that he was reading Byron's mood correctly. "Make sure you take care of yourself."

"I'll try. Night, Pete."

8: The Dad Who Cried Wolf

Byron

IF NOTHING ELSE, at nine thirty p.m. on New Year's Eve, the motorways were clear, only the occasional HGV charging through the night, the custom cab lights lending a festive ambience that went some way towards lifting Byron out of his melancholy.

He'd stayed long enough to hear the news and play the part of supportive son and sibling, and he had a plan in his head for when the time came, but he was too angry, too sad, too heartsick to do more. This was going to impact on his NQT year and likely mean starting over—maybe even finding another job—but he wouldn't know until Thursday, when he'd be back in school and could speak to the headteacher.

For now, he tried to set it aside and concentrate on his driving, which was harder without having to negotiate with other motorway users. His thoughts kept returning to the arguments earlier that day, when he'd done as Pete asked and taken care of himself, but had it been at his mum's and sisters' expense? They'd wanted him to stay, done everything to make it impossible for him to leave. In a family as screwed up as theirs, begging with tears made a pleasant change, and in the past, he'd believed every word.

Back in uni, the counsellor on campus had got him to 'unpack the narrative', figure out what was true and false, and where his accountability began and ended. It had taken a few sessions— actually, a *lot* of sessions—before something finally clicked into place. Like looking through new glasses, the world appeared

DEBBIE MCGOWAN

strange, the ground sloping precariously beneath his feet, yet substantially clearer than before. He didn't owe his parents for his upbringing; they'd chosen to have children, and it was their responsibility to take care of him and his sisters. That was it. No payback required. No need for guilt or gratitude. His only obligation was to himself and to those he chose to care about. Byron had tried to get his sisters to understand or, better still, go and see counsellors themselves, but they'd refused, acted as if he was the one being unreasonable, and today, they'd fully taken their mum's side.

So here he was, the son deserting his family when they needed him most. The new enemy. Every junction he passed, he debated turning off and going back, but then he thought about Pete waiting for him at the jazz club and how happy he'd sounded when Byron said he'd get there, somehow. He wasn't quite going to make it for ten; the satnav gave an ETA of 22:11, so not too late. Even so, imagining Pete checking the time and watching the door had Byron pushing the speed limit as much as he dared.

New Year's Eve wasn't the ideal time to go into it, but he was ready. If tonight was their first official date, and it felt like it was, then it was only fair Pete knew what was what, even if that meant it was their *only* date.

At last, Byron turned off the motorway, heading along roads populated with colourfully lit houses, strings of lights swaying in trees, inflatable Santas, families of reindeer—mums, dads and babies in perfect festive harmony, reflecting what existed behind many of those front doors with their wreaths of holly and mistletoe. Once upon a time, Byron had a taste of that life, thanks to his grandparents taking care of their 'little virtuoso'. No favouritism—they'd doted on all three grandchildren—and Byron had felt loved, treasured. Perhaps he and Pete were destined only to be friends, but because

72

of Pete, Byron was prepared to take a chance at finding that life again.

The satnav's announcement that he'd reached his destination came at 22:04, and he was delighted he'd made up a few minutes, although it wasn't enough time to drive home and walk back. He stopped in the first empty parking space he found, which was a way further down the opposite side of the street, and checked the restrictions: he was fine for this evening but would have to move the car before six a.m., so that put paid to getting drunk, which was probably a good thing. He'd also have to leave talking to Pete, as the music coming from the jazz bar was loud enough for Byron to recognise the current piece as 'One for My Baby'. It became louder still when the door opened, and out walked Pete, phone in hand. Byron's chest filled with butterflies at the sight of him, so much so that he didn't immediately register the vibrations emanating from his pocket. He took out his phone and hit 'answer'.

"Hey."

"Hey. How are you doing?"

"Good. You?"

"Yeah. I'm good too. I'm, er...missing you?"

Byron couldn't have stopped himself smiling if his life depended on it. "I'd say I'm missing you too, except..." He paused to cross the road. "You're right here."

For a second, Pete stared, a bit dazed, his phone still clamped to his ear. Byron advanced, cheeks burning, pulse racing, more nervous than ever before, but he was determined he would do this. He stepped up to Pete, who barely had a chance to lower his arm before Byron wrapped him in a hug and kissed him solidly on the lips.

"I did miss you today," he murmured, unwilling to move away when it had taken all his courage to get to this moment. "So much."

"Me too." Pete's words buzzed like electrical current from the point of contact, sending little shudders of sensation all through Byron's body.

"Can we talk?"

"Yeah, sure."

Byron released Pete from the hug, and Pete put his phone away, taking Byron's hand as he led the way on shaky legs back to his car. Once they were both seated with the doors shut, he switched on the engine and the heating.

"Are you cold?" Pete asked.

"I'm not sure."

"You're shivering." Pete reached over and reinstated his grip on Byron's hand. "It's OK, you know. You don't owe me an explanation."

"I want to tell you everything. There are things you need to know about my family...and me. If we're going to do this." Byron lifted their joined hands.

"I'm listening," Pete said and lightly squeezed Byron's fingers.

Where to begin? He'd had the same dilemma in his first appointment with the counsellor, but it was different this time because it was about Pete's well-being as much as his own, and because fate, karma, poetic justice, the wrath of God or whatever had intervened.

"When you asked why I turned down the Royal Conservatoire, it was because of my dad. The music—it's not even part of me. It *is* me. When I was little, my dad was always having a go at me about rushing my homework and not earning my pocket money. He said music wasn't a proper job, it was a hobby, and for ages, I thought that was why he had a problem with it.

"My grandparents stood up for me. They paid for my music lessons, bought my instruments, took me to concerts and were there for my exams and performances. They'd have loved Carols by Candlelight, whether I was in it or not. They were the best people. I don't even want to think what would've happened to me without them.

"When I asked if you'd come to hear my solo, that was when I realised how much you mean to me, and it scares me because... Well, the thing is, my dad is mentally ill—or evil. It's hard to know for sure, but either way, the effect's been the same on all of us. I don't know if his parents are still alive, or if he has any siblings. His parents disowned him, and my mum and her parents felt sorry for him. My mum still does, which was how she was able to forgive him, but I can't.

"After my gran died, I tried so hard to stand up to him, to keep doing music. I applied to music colleges and was offered places at all of them. He was livid, but he never hit me. He never hurt any of us physically. What he did..."

Byron took a moment to breathe, aware his anger wasn't far beneath the surface and that he was crushing Pete's hand. He eased off. "Sorry."

"It's OK." Pete flexed his fingers a few times and took Byron's hand again. "We can continue this another time if you want."

"No. I'd rather get it out the way if that's all right?"

"Of course."

Byron inhaled deeply, exhaled slowly, and picked up where he'd left off. "After I was offered the place at the Royal Conservatoire, my dad told us he had bowel cancer, stage four, which is terminal, so the doctors weren't treating it, just managing his pain. So, I thought, OK. I'll defer my place for a year or however long he's got left, but he said he didn't want that. He hoped I'd grant a dying man his last wish, and that was to see his son become a scientist. Because of him, I'd taken physics and chemistry A' Levels, so I applied to uni and followed that path to here.

"As it turned out, he didn't actually have cancer. There was nothing wrong with him, or not with his body, anyway. Even the 'music is a hobby' thing was a lie. It was about me stealing the attention he used to get from my grandparents. Narcissism—a personality disorder of some sort. That's what the counsellor I saw at uni reckoned. Dad did the same to Anna—my younger sister. She's a super-talented artist, but his 'dying wish' was for her to study something that would give her a career and mean she was never put in the situation Mum and Emily were of depending on a man who'd only let them down."

"Emily's your older sister?" Pete asked.

"Who married a Protestant, yes. And her husband's a really nice guy. Again, Dad's issues are nothing to do with Tom being a Protestant. He hates that he stole Emily's attention. After Anna and I went off to uni…I'm not sure what happened exactly, but Emily was pregnant, so maybe she'd been to see the doctor and mentioned Dad's illness or something. Whatever, Mum found out he'd been lying all along, yet she stayed with him."

"Wow."

"I know. I still can't get my head around it. That was when I stopped going home. I hadn't seen him or Mum for four years until last summer, when they turned up at Anna's graduation ceremony. She'd only invited Emily and me, and actually, Anna and I got a restraining order after Dad threatened us and said he'd make sure we both finished our degrees, whatever it took. I'm not the sort of person to cause a scene ever, but especially not at my sister's graduation, so I was civil to him, which Mum took as a sign that we'd resolved our differences. She thought I'd be home for Christmas and promised he wouldn't be there. Well, that turned out to be a lie too, but I didn't go home."

"I had a feeling you spent Christmas alone," Pete said.

"It wasn't awful."

"Really?"

Byron shrugged and laced his fingers through Pete's. "We've kind of had our own Christmas these past few days, haven't we?"

Pete smiled. "Yeah, we have."

"I still worry I pushed you into playing."

"You encouraged me, By. That's different to pushing. Is that what you meant about being scared? You think you're doing what your dad did?"

Byron nodded, not trusting himself to speak. He'd expected he'd need to explain, but Pete understood where he was coming from.

"Well, that's a massive thing, isn't it? But you've told me now, so I can protect myself if I have to, but the Byron Walker I've come to know over the past month? He's nothing like the man you've just described. Do you believe me?"

Byron nodded again. He could gladly have fallen into Pete's arms and sobbed but stoically swallowed the lump in his throat so he could conclude his tale. "Yesterday, my dad was diagnosed with cancer for real, and it is terminal. Mum went with him to the oncologist. He's got a few months, a year maybe. I agreed to go home closer to the end and help out. I don't know when that will be."

If Pete was thinking the same as Byron—that his dad had received his just desserts—he didn't voice it. He leaned across the centre console, placed the gentlest kiss on Byron's cheek, and said, "Whatever you need, I'm here for you."

"Thank you." Byron switched off the engine, preparing to leave the car and start their New Year's Eve date, albeit with only an hour of the old year left on the clock. The burden was still heavy on his shoulders, and he doubted he'd ever stop worrying that he was his father's son, but Pete's assurance gave him hope, and that was enough for now.

"You know," Pete said as they walked, hand in hand, back to the jazz bar, "I spend every Christmas complaining about how awful my family is, and I'm not bragging or comparing here, but yesterday, I realised how lucky I am."

"Why? What happened yesterday?"

"Short version? My mum approves of you."

"We've never even spoken."

"I know, but if we want to do our own thing next Christmas, we have her blessing."

"Next Christmas is a long way off." And Byron's dad would still be hanging on, no doubt, making sure he spread his misery for as long as possible.

As they neared the doors to the bar, Pete stopped walking. "How do you feel about public displays of affection?"

"Um…OK, I guess?"

"Good. Because I really want to snog you right now. May I?"

Byron laughed, nervous, excited, and nodded his consent, sliding his arms under Pete's as he was reeled in, and they snogged beneath a blue neon light to a sultry, bassy accompaniment of 'What Are You Doing New Year's Eve?'

Epilogue:
Carols by Candle and Torchlight

Pete

IT'S HEAVING!" CHARLIE remarked unnecessarily as she and Pete were shuffled along in the unruly line of people outside Black Hole Studios—the venue for this year's Carols by Candlelight. "Is that why it's here instead of at the church?"

"I don't think so. There was a fire at St. Mark's last week."

"Oh, really? Caused by a candle, by any chance?"

"An electrical fault, Byron said."

They moved a few steps closer to the door. Charlie went up on tiptoes, peering over the multitude. "I've been to stadium gigs with smaller crowds."

Pete shook his head, chuckling at her exaggeration, although he didn't recall there being this many people the last time he'd been to Carols by Candlelight—back when he was in the school orchestra. Still, it wasn't long before they were through the doors and being ushered into the auditorium, a giant black box of a room with rows of seats already half full of people chatting to their neighbours. Pete swallowed in an attempt to pop his ears, except air pressure wasn't the problem.

"I think I've figured out why they call this place Black Hole," he said, and he might just as well have said nothing at all. The room's acoustics swallowed his words. Ahead of him, Charlie was moving along a row of seats halfway to the stage, and Pete quickly dodged in behind her, nearly bumping into her when she stopped midway, putting them smack-bang in the middle of the auditorium.

Disconcerted—he was more of an edge person—Pete took his seat and occupied himself with watching the place fill with parishioners from the various churches, performers' proud parents and fellow pupils, many decked out in Christmas hats and sweaters, jangling festive earrings and temporary necklaces of tinsel. Soon the black box was a mass of colour and sparkles, and as the house lights dimmed, the stage lit up, glowing and flickering with what appeared to be hundreds of candles. Pete tingled with the familiar and much-missed excitement he'd felt as a kid watching the sky for Santa's sleigh. This was a special night, overflowing with the spirit of the season, an entire community celebrating together.

There were no announcements before the first bunch of primary school kids marched out and assumed their positions, nor did they need any for their rousing rendition of 'Go Tell It on the Mountain'. What they lacked in tunefulness they more than made up for in enthusiasm, and by the last chorus the audience was clapping and singing along and applauded loudly, whooping and whistling, as the little ones took their bows and filed off one side of the stage while the next group came on from the other.

So it went on, smoothly rotating through all the primary schools. The children were absolute stars—actual stars in the case of Pete's old school, who sang 'Christmas Star' with such beautiful harmonies and choreography that Pete could've thumped Charlie for ruining the moment to 'whisper' in his ear, "Mrs. Hardacre's still working her magic, then."

He had to smile, though, because as soon as Charlie had said it, he'd spotted Mrs. Hardacre conducting her little stars from her usual cross-legged, unobtrusive position in front of the stage. She'd taught Year Six in Charlie's and Pete's time and had to be nearing retirement age, yet she was the same as ever. He had to wonder if she and Mr. Hardacre had discussions like his and Byron's over the past few months.

At times, they'd come dangerously close to arguments, Pete's perspective being that, like Mrs. Hardacre, Byron was wasting his talents on teaching. He understood now that it was far more complex than Byron not having the guts to follow his dreams even though he would be free of obligation once his dad died, assuming he ever did. The previous week, he'd gone into a hospice for end-of-life care, which was promising—and Pete was definitely going to hell for thinking that, but it seemed like it was the least the man could do after everything he'd put his family through.

He hadn't shared that sentiment with Byron, obviously. Byron hated his dad, but as Pete's mum had pointed out when he told her what was going on, hate was as strong an emotion as love, and Pete would do Byron no favours by fanning the flames that would, eventually, extinguish themselves. Time, patience and understanding. That was what he could give to Byron, even though it meant spending Christmas apart again this year because Byron's family needed him.

Meanwhile, come Sunday afternoon, the Davenports would all descend on Ben's big house in the country, and for once, Pete wasn't complaining. In fact, Byron's situation made Pete more thankful than ever that he was part of a loving family. There were fights, sure, and if fibs were snowflakes they'd have a white Christmas every year. But there was no gaslighting or emotional blackmail. They were all free to choose their own paths, and if they got it wrong, there was always someone who'd put the kettle on and listen or lecture them over a cup of tea before setting them off on the right track again.

"Hey, hey, here he is!" Charlie jabbed her elbow into Pete's side, annoyingly, although he'd daydreamed his way through who knew how many performances, and he'd have missed Byron's performance too. Or not his specifically. He was one of the band and on bass guitar tonight, along with a pianist and keyboard player, accompanying a Year Seven female soloist who had the audience rapt from the very first note of Amy Grant's 'Breath of Heaven'. As Pete stood with everyone else to deliver a standing ovation, he and Byron locked gazes, and Pete nodded and smiled. The singer had been every bit as good as Byron had said.

That was the thing about being with Byron Walker. It was a constant lesson in humility, for as talented as he was, he was the kind of person who wanted everyone to shine. What he'd said a year ago, 'Those who can, do', wasn't wrong, but not everyone was equipped to 'do' and 'teach'. Byron inspired those kids, to the extent that Our Lady's Church choir now boasted thirty members and Pete and Byron were no longer the only under-forties. The way things were going, they wouldn't be singing in the gallery for much longer. It was already creaking under the strain.

Byron was brilliant in so many ways, yet he doubted himself constantly over every little thing. It could be frustrating, reassuring him—*yes, I want to see that film; no, you didn't push me into agreeing to pizza*—whatever they were doing, and Pete wasn't convinced he always handled it right, but after being together for almost a year, he knew with certainty that he would deal with Byron's insecurity all day every day for the rest of eternity if the alternative was not having him in his life.

The interval followed Moor Croft's ensemble piece— the school choir would conclude the evening—and Charlie went off to chat to someone, while Pete stepped outside to clear his head, not expecting to see Byron until the end. However, he and some of the other teachers were shepherding groups of students out to the car park to be picked up by their parents. Perhaps it was due to the change of venue because it hadn't been like that in Pete's day, which really wasn't that long ago. Curious, he wandered over so he could walk back in with Byron.

"Hey. What's going on?"

Byron shrugged. "Child Protection issue. I'm not sure what, but the repercussions are pretty huge. The head of music says Mr. Lewis will need a DBS check."

"Ohhh. He's not gonna like that."

"No, but if he doesn't agree to it, I'll have to pull the students out of the church choir, which he'll like even less. Anyway, sorry, but I've got to go. See you later." Byron gave Pete a quick kiss and dashed off, presumably to the backstage area, and Pete returned to the auditorium, where Charlie was already in her seat and looked at him quizzically.

"Where did you go?"

"To get some air."

She sniffed. "You went to see Byron."

"I didn't *go* to see him, but I did see him. How d'you know?"

"His cologne. I can smell it on you. Doesn't it set off your allergies?"

"Nope." Not all scents did, thank goodness. There would be nothing less romantic than bursting into hives every time his boyfriend kissed him. Pete was about to ask who Charlie had been talking to but was cut off when the lights blinked out, leaving the auditorium in complete darkness other than the green fire exit signs. Then, in the centre of the stage, a tiny flickering light appeared and a solo voice began to sing about one little candle. Pete hadn't heard the song before, but it had a gospel feel to it, and sure enough, more candles and voices joined in, then more, until there were three distinct rows of candles and behind each a singing head, which was a bit ghastly, Pete thought, even if those heads sang wonderfully.

He revised that assessment when the lights came back on and he checked the programme, discovering he'd been admiring St. Mark's Church choir, which he couldn't do on principle, and not because they were C of E. Increasingly, mostly on Byron's behalf, he was irked that Our Lady's choir wasn't part of this celebration, and it marred his enjoyment of the rest of the evening so that he was marking time until Moor Croft's performance. As if to add insult to injury, Moor Croft's choir was joined by the Methodist church's bell ringers, whose smug grins as they ding-donged the intro to 'Carol of the Bells' had Pete wanting to shove their rotten bells up their noses.

The choir, though…Pete was blown away. The swell and retreat of their combined voices was like a heart beating, so perfectly in sync, far and away the best of all the choirs in Pete's opinion. And yes, the bells were good too. He was so swept up in the experience, it was a while before he thought to look for Byron, and it was no easy task when he was one tenor in a choir of fifty, all dressed in uniform black shirts and pants. Pete scanned each row, right to left, front to back, panicking slightly that something had happened backstage that meant Byron wasn't there at all, but there he was at last: third from the end of the back row. And once Pete found him, he saw only him. That was the moment he knew for sure he was 100% besotted with Byron Walker.

✽✽✽

Byron

RELUCTANTLY, BYRON REMOVED his gloves and flicked through his hymnal. Between the dark of the church hall and his steamed-up glasses, it made little difference if he was on the right page; he'd sung it often enough to know it by heart anyway.

"With respect, Mr. Lewis," Councillor Bob tried, but their cantankerous choirmaster was having none of it and began banging out the intro to 'In The Bleak Midwinter' on the increasingly tuneless piano.

Norman leaned in and muttered, "I think he's finally lost it."

Byron nodded in agreement. The power cut had happened as they were arriving for choir practice, and it had taken out every Christmas light in the neighbourhood, but at that point, no-one was bothered. A couple of times a month, the power would go off for a few minutes and then come back on, and to start with, it had been kind of fun singing by the light of their phones' LEDs, although it would've been more so if Pete had been here instead of at his work's Christmas do. For all Byron knew, he was passed out face down in a plate of turkey and gravy, but he couldn't even text, as the LED had drained his phone in five minutes flat, and everyone else's had followed suit, blipping out one by one.

Good old Norman had come to the rescue with one of those handy emergency lights, which he kept fully charged in his car; an hour on, even that was growing dim, and the church hall was bitterly cold. Yet Mr. Lewis insisted they kept going. Byron couldn't make sense of it—not just the singing in the dark. It wasn't as if someone was forcing Mr. Lewis to turn up every Thursday and Sunday, unless Mrs. Lewis was even more of a tyrant than her husband, which didn't seem possible. So why did he do it? Granted, there weren't many people who could play the organ—was it out of obligation? And if so, did that obligation extend to being choirmaster, or could the two roles be separated?

It had been on Byron's mind for a while—well, it wouldn't have occurred to him at all, but Pete put it out there one Thursday after practice, when they were in the pub, and a few of the others said it was a great idea. Byron had told them there was no way on earth he was doing it, end of discussion, except the seed had been planted, and the harder he tried to *not* think about it, the more he wondered… Could he? *Should* he?

On the few occasions one of them—usually Norman— had thrown down any kind of gauntlet, like suggesting some of the tenors sing the soprano part when the soprano section was short, Mr. Lewis would kick up a stink but then usually go with it. This was different, though, and despite Pete's and everyone else's contention that Mr. Lewis could 'only say no', he could actually say 'no, you can't take over my choir. Get out!' That was a risk Byron couldn't take, but at the same time—

"Mr. Walker, are you with us?"

"Yes. Sorry, Mr. Lewis." He had no idea what he'd missed.

"I was going to ask you and Mr. Davenport to duet this Sunday, seeing as the two of you get along so splendidly." Mr. Lewis's grimace-smile shone particularly grimly through the gloom. "But as he's once again decided not to bless us with his presence, I'll have to give it to Mr.—"

Cut short by the sudden brightness of all the hall lights coming on at once, Mr. Lewis swore. Byron, and doubtless everyone else, instinctively shut his eyes, then experimentally opened one, squinting through his lashes at Pete, who sauntered over, cool as a rosy-cheeked cucumber, tugging off his scarf and grinning broadly.

"Evening all. Sorry I'm so late. I, er...got into a fight with a cardboard compactor." He took up his position to Byron's right and glanced at the hymnal. "The power's been back on for ages, by the way—I reset the hall's RCD on my way in. Did I hear something about a duet?"

Byron caught a whiff of beer on Pete's breath and gave him a look that he hoped conveyed *you're being too loud*, although it was fun to see Pete in such a merry mood.

"Indeed you did." Mr. Lewis beckoned to Byron and Pete *cheerfully*. Indeed, the transformation was astonishing, as if the return of the understated fluorescent-tubed lighting in the church hall had miraculously cast out years of pent-up misery, *and* he was smiling. "I believe you're familiar with this one, Peter." He began to play the gentle 6/8 arpeggios of 'O Holy Night', watching Pete with what Byron could only describe as fondness.

"I do," Pete confirmed, smiling. To Byron, he said, "My first solo."

"You kept that quiet."

"Yeah. I messed it up."

"He sang very well," Mr. Lewis contended, and before Pete could argue the contrary raised his head to bring him in. The colour shot from Pete's cheeks to his ears, and he glanced nervously at Byron, but he hit that first phrase perfectly and continued singing as they moved around to stand either side of Mr. Lewis and read the score. Byron stood to the right so he could also turn the pages and almost missed a couple, too enthralled with Pete. He sang with so much feeling and musicality, Byron was honoured to offer his harmony and almost in tears as the final note drew to a close and the rest of the choir applauded. He couldn't be sure, but he thought a couple of the altos may well have been crying too, while Norman beamed at them proudly and hugged them both when they re-joined the ranks.

"Thank you, gentlemen," Mr. Lewis said, closing the piano lid and standing. "An excellent and fitting offertory for Fourth Sunday. Now, I have an announcement to make—good news perhaps. As you know, Mrs. Lewis is a high-up in the NHS, and she has a new job in the southwest, which means this is our last Christmas at Our Lady's."

Everyone made the right kinds of sounds—"Oh, no," "Sorry you're leaving," and, "Well done, Mrs. Lewis."

Mr. Lewis patted the air with his hands—a signal for them all to quieten down. "Thank you. I realise I haven't always been the easiest chap to get along with..."

Pete murmured, "No kidding!" Norman snorted into his hymnal. Several of the altos wheezed.

"...but it's been my privilege to play for you and lead you this past thirty years. Believe it or not, I was the same age as young Messrs Davenport and Walker here when I took up the mantle."

Byron glanced sideways at Pete to find him doing the same. It was a comforting thought that they might still be here in another thirty years.

"So, no choir practice next week, of course, but the first of the New Year, I'll introduce you to your new organist. I say new—Mrs. Rita Jones has attended this church almost as long as I have, and she's delighted to finally get her hands and feet on my…er…"

It was too late for Mr. Lewis to pull out of that nosedive. The choir was a singular heap of hysterical laughter. He took it well, despite looking like his head might explode from all the blood fuelling a blush to end all blushes. Eventually, though, they all settled enough for him to finish his little speech.

"Mrs. Jones is a competent organist and accompanist, but she has no experience with choirs, so I'm afraid you may have to muddle through for a few weeks, but Father Benson and I do have someone in mind. Again, thank you, all, for your hard work—in particularly adverse conditions this evening. I'll see you on Sunday, ten sharp."

"Come to the pub with us!" Carol called.

"Yes, do!" Norman seconded. "Let us buy you a pint."

"Oh, I—"

"Come on," Pete said. "You can't leave without a celebration."

"Well, if you insist…"

"We do!" several voices said at once.

"All right then. I'll follow you over as soon as I've checked in with Mrs. Lewis and locked up."

Satisfied with that and in blithe spirits, people gathered their belongings, and the adults headed out.

Byron checked his phone and groaned when the screen didn't respond. In all the revelry, he'd forgotten it was out of juice. "What time is it?" he asked Pete.

"Just before nine."

"OK. Parents should be here soon."

"Mr. Walker, a word, please?"

"Yes, Mr. Lewis. Pete, you can go—"

"Or I can wait." He didn't move. Byron shrugged and turned to Mr. Lewis, who smiled disarmingly.

"I saw the exceptional work you did with your students at the Carols by Candlelight. Then there're all these youngsters you've brought in. Our Lady's needs someone like you, who can build bridges with the local community. To that end, I've recommended you to Father Benson as the new choirmaster. I hope you don't mind."

Byron heard the young choristers whoop and say, "Get in there, Mr. W!" but he kept his cool even though there was some kind of party going on in his chest.

"Not at all. Thank you, Mr. Lewis. I appreciate your confidence in me."

Mr. Lewis nodded demurely and went off on his rounds, checking all the windows and doors other than the main entrance were secure.

"Well," Pete said. "Well, well."

"Hmm."

"You don't sound very excited."

"I am," Byron said, and he was, truly. He was still struggling to accept that music could be more than 'just a hobby', but he was finally doing something with it—playing and singing with others instead of practising alone—and he was helping young people develop their talents.

The parents of some of those young people arrived to collect them, and Byron and Pete followed them out, making sure everyone got away safely before the two of them headed for the pub next door.

"What's the 'but'?" Pete asked.

Byron shrugged. "I want to do it, but you're more important."

"And *I* want you to do it, so what's the problem?"

"Christmas. If I take on the choir, we'll never get to spend it together."

"Because you've got to be here."

"Uh-huh."

"Right." Pete stopped walking and spun Byron to face him, gently scragging him by the front of his coat. "Then I guess I have to be here too, seeing as yesterday I told my family this would be the last Christmas you and I spend apart."

The End

About the Author

Debbie McGowan is an author and publisher based in a semi-rural corner of Lancashire, England. She writes character-driven, realist fiction, celebrating life, love and relationships. A working-class girl, she 'ran away' to London at seventeen, was homeless, unemployed and then homeless again, interspersed with animal rights activism (all legal, honest ;)) and volunteer work as a mental health advocate. At twenty-five, she went back to college to study social science—tough with two toddlers, but they had a 'stay at home' dad, so it worked itself out. These days, the toddlers are young women (much to their chagrin) and Debbie teaches undergraduate students, writes novels and runs an independent publishing company, occasionally grabbing an hour's sleep where she can.

Social Media Links

Website: debbiemcgowan.co.uk and hidingbehindthecouch.com
Newsletter Signup: eepurl.com/b8emHL
Blog: deb248211.blogspot.com
Facebook: facebook.com/DebbieMcGowanAuthor and facebook.com/beatentrackpublishing
Twitter: @writerdebmcg
YouTube: youtube.com/deb248211
Instagram: instagram/writerdebmcg
Tumblr: writerdebmcg.tumblr.com
LinkedIn: uk.linkedin.com/in/writerdebmcg
Goodreads: goodreads.com/DebbieMcGowan
Books2Read: books2read.com/DebbieMcGowan

By the Author

I'm not a single-genre author, for which I make no apology. Nor do I write stories of a specific length; I believe a story should be as long as it needs to be.

Thus, to assist you in navigating my catalogue, I've also included the closest-fitting genres and types of publication.

Hiding Behind The Couch Series
(Contemporary/Literary Fiction)
The ongoing story of 'The Circle'…
Nine friends from high school;
Nine friends for life.

The Story So Far…
(in chronological order)

- *Beginnings* (Novella)
- *Ruminations* (Novel)
- *Class-A* (Short Story – also in *Take a Chance* anthology)
- *Hiding Behind The Couch* (Season One)
- *No Time Like The Present* (Season Two)
- *The Harder They Fall* (Season Three)
- *Crying in the Rain* (Novel)
- *First Christmas* (Novella)
- *In The Stars Part I: Capricorn–Gemini* (Season Four)
- *Breaking Waves* (Novella)
- *Chain of Secrets* (Novella – also in Love Unlocked anthology)
- *In The Stars Part II: Cancer–Sagittarius* (Season Five)
- *A Midnight Clear* (Novella – also in *Boughs of Evergreen* anthology)
- *Red Hot Christmas* (Novella)

- *Two By Two* (Season Six)
- *Hiding Out* (Novella – CHO Crossover)
- *Those Jeffries Boys* (Novel)
- *The WAG and The Scoundrel* (Gray Fisher #1)
- **Perfect Tenor (Novella)**
- *The Lost Mitten* (see 'Children's Stories')
- *Reunions* (Season Seven)
- *Tabula Rasa* (Gray Fisher #2)
- *Breakfast at Cordelia's Aquarium* (Short Story)
- *Reverberations* (Novel)
- *To Be Sure* (Novella – also in *Never Too Late* anthology)
- *What A Scorcher!* (Flash Fiction)
- *Goth of Christmas Past* (Front of House #1)
- *The Advent of Reason* (Novella)
- *Not My Christmas* (Novella)
- *Highlights* ~ co-written with A.M. Leibowitz (Short Story – Notes from Boston meets Hiding Behind The Couch)
- *Distractions* (Gray Fisher #3)

Checking Him Out Series
(M/M and LGBTQ Romance)

- *Checking Him Out* (Book One)
- *Checking Him Out For the Holidays* (Novella)
- *Hiding Out* (Novella – Noah and Matty – HBTC Crossover)
- *Taking Him On* (Book Two – Noah and Matty)
- *Checking In* (Book Three)
- *The Making of Us* (Book Four – Jesse and Leigh)

Seeds of Tyrone Series
(M/M Romance)

~ co-written with Raine O'Tierney

- *Leaving Flowers* (Book One)
- *Where the Grass is Greener* (Book Two)
- *Christmas Craic and Mistletoe* (Book Three)

Stand-Alone Stories

- *Champagne* (LGBTQ Historical Novel)
- 'Time to Go' (Contemporary Short in *Story Salon Big Book of Stories*)
- *And The Walls Came Tumbling Down* (Sci-fi Novel)
- *No Dice* (Sci-fi Novel)
- *Double Six* (Sci-fi Novel)
- *Sugar and Sawdust* (M/M Romance Short Story)
- *Cherry Pop Valentine* (M/M Romance Short Story)
- *Coming Up* ~ co-written with Al Stewart (LGBTQ Short Story)
- *Of the Bauble* (LGBTQ Fantasy Romance Novella)
- *So Long, Little Black Diamonds* (True Short Story)
- *The Pastor's Last Drop* (Ongoing Historical Novel – Wattpad)
- *When Skies Have Fallen* (LGBTQ Historical Romance Novel)
- *A Snowy Ball* (When Skies Have Fallen Novelette)
- *The Great Village Bun Fight* (LGBTQ Comedy Novella – also in *Seasons of Love* anthology)
- 'Oh No She Didn't!' (LGBTQ Short Story in *Upstaged!: an anthology of women who love women in the performing arts*)
- *The Great Pretendo* (Flash Fiction)
- 'Nina, Pretty Ballerina' (Short Story in *Play On…: a collection of short stories, poetry and prose, inspired by the songs of ABBA*)
- *Meredith's Dagger* (Contemporary/Historical Feminist/LGBTQ Novel)

Audiobooks

- *And The Walls Came Tumbling Down* – Narrated by Hannibal Mills
- *Checking Him Out* – Narrated by Tim Larkfield
- *Of The Bauble* – Narrated by Jack Hardman
- *The Great Village Bun Fight* – Narrated by Jack Hardman
- *When Skies Have Fallen* – Narrated by Tim Holbourne

Children's Stories (written as J.S. Morley)

- *The Lost Mitten* ~ illustrated by Sofia Oxelstrand
- *Chompy the Velociraptor* ~ illustrated by Kate Andrew
- *Zoom the Pterodactyl*

www.debbiemcgowan.co.uk

Beaten Track Publishing

For more titles from Beaten Track Publishing,
please visit our website:

https://www.beatentrackpublishing.com

Thanks for reading!